RUB

RUB

A Heavenly Story With an Earthly Beginning

ROBERT S. BONHEIM

Rub

Copyright © 2019 by Robert S. Bonheim. All rights reserved.

No part of this publication may be reproduced, stored in a retrieval system or transmitted in any way by any means, electronic, mechanical, photocopy, recording or otherwise without the prior permission of the author except as provided by USA copyright law.

The opinions expressed by the author are not necessarily those of URLink Print and Media.

1603 Capitol Ave., Suite 310 Cheyenne, Wyoming USA 82001
1-888-980-6523 | admin@urlinkpublishing.com

URLink Print and Media is committed to excellence in the publishing industry.

Book design copyright © 2019 by URLink Print and Media. All rights reserved.

Published in the United States of America

ISBN 978-1-64367-716-3 (Paperback)
ISBN 978-1-64367-717-0 (Digital)

Biblical Fiction
12.08.19

CONTENTS

Chapter 1: Questions 7
Chapter 2: Paradise Above 14
Chapter 3: Special Place 21
Chapter 4: Revelation 28
Chapter 5: To The Session 36
Chapter 6: The First Session 43
Chapter 7: The Beginning 50
Chapter 8: The Red-Covered Bible 57
Chapter 9: Robert and Jeni 65
Chapter 10: Another Session 74
Chapter 11: Understanding 84
Chapter 12: Curious 93

Book II

Chapter 13: Jerusha 105
Chapter 14: The Banquet 110
Chapter 15: Regrets 120
Chapter 16: College 127
Chapter 17: Secrets 133
Chapter 18: Pregnant 139
Chapter 19: Decision 144

Chapter 20: More Secrets..150
Chapter 21: Special Decisions...162
Chapter 22: Another Decision 172
Chapter 23: Do Right..177
Chapter 24: No Wedding...192
Chapter 25: Robert...196
Chapter 26: The Wedding 200
Chapter 27: Hawaii 203

CHAPTER 1

Questions

What kind of a place is this? I've never seen anything like it. In fact, what am I doing here? Thousands of thoughts are bombarding my brain. I don't recall coming here. Strangely, I do not even know who I am. I don't recall anything before this time, right now. In somewhat of a questionable way, I'm not sure that I understand what I am thinking, yet, I talk audibly and understand what I say.

How strange this place is. Yet, it seems to be very special. It is silent all around. I can almost hear my own thoughts as if they were speaking out loud. An aurora of solitude permeates the air embracing my very being. I continued to survey my surroundings. But I could not stop thinking nor questioning. Where is this place and what is it? How did I get here and, most of all, who am I? Who am I, yes, who am I? If I only knew who I was, perhaps all of this would make sense to me. No answers came. I resigned myself to take it all from here and began searching for the answers.

With all these perplexing thoughts racing through my mind, I failed to notice the brightness of the entire area. All the surroundings were illuminated with a light of utter brilliance. Nothing escaped its presence, as it appeared to come from a distant place. I could see the general area and direction from which it originated but I could not actually see it. Everything was unexplainable. All of this, at least for me, was a mystery. It was completely incomprehensible. Through the solitude of the quietness I could detect music, far off, but so near, softly filling the air. What soothing music. Comforting strains of melodious sounds rang in my ears. The air was exhilarating to breathe. There was freshness, a pureness about it. Each breath seemed to empower me with life and energy. Something else about this air readily caught my attention. It had an undeniable scent. It was perfumed with the fragrance of the honeysuckle flower. How did I know that? I don't know. I just did…that's funny.

What a curious place this is. I am baffled. I know not a thing about myself, why I'm here, or even what this place might be. Nevertheless, I am beginning to feel at home here in this beautiful place.

The light about me was constant. It radiated gold like, rays that lit up all the surroundings. It appeared to light up even the very perfumed air that I was breathing. It gave everything a golden quality. I was deeply amazed at what I saw and was now experiencing.

Then, gazing off into a distant place, I noticed a form moving towards me, moving at a rapid pace. As the form drew nearer, I could see that the form, whoever or whatever it was, looked somewhat like me. But of a truth I wasn't quite sure what I really looked like. I had seen a reflection of myself from the pond of clear water that was located just to the side of me. I would occasionally glance there to see if it was still I staring up out of the shinning water. No other form was there, only mine. What a curious form it was. Somewhat straight was the bulk of the form supported by two pillars, with two thinner flexible pillars like extensions protruding from the upper sides of its body. Upon the top of that body was perched an even thinner pillar a round like object with various features that appeared to give the whole form various abilities and functions. The form was wrapped in some kind of red like cloth or garment, and around the middle there was a small thin white girdle. I suppose it was there to keep that cloth from falling off the form. I saw myself mirrored in the watery pond. I was a mysterious form in a mysterious place.

It did not seem very long, but that form that I saw in the distance was now very close to me. What should I do? Should I stay right here, or should I leave and go somewhere? I was perplexed. If I left, where would I go? I did not even know where I was. Besides, how do I know if even I could leave this place? By the time I was to make a decision on whether to leave or stay, the form was standing right in front of me. "Hello there," the form quietly but firmly greeted me.

"How are you?" said the form with a smile. I could not respond at all. This form actually talked to me with words that I could hear. I even knew what was said, and amazingly I understood every word.

"Are you all right? Can you talk to me?" the form asked me in an assuring way.

I still could not speak. It was as if something inside me caused me to be stiff and immoveable. I wasn't frightened, nor did I feel intimidated. I just was so dumb-founded that I remained speechless. The form, which looked almost like me, was patient, continually looking and talking to me saying, "Now take your time. I am here to help you. It is understandable that all of this is so confusing to you."

I could sense that there was help being offered to me by this strange form. I wanted to respond. There were so many things upon my mind. There were so many questions. There was so much to know. I just had to speak. This was the only option I had; I need to take advantage of the situation before this form left me.

"Please, talk to me. Don't be frightened," urged the form. "I am here to help you. Now, again, how are you?" I heard that question again. "I'm fine," I heard myself say aloud. I heard my own voice responding with words I knew this form understood. Amazing, I actually spoke audible words!

"I believe that I am fine," I heard myself saying and thinking whatever that means. The form looked at me with a knowing look and replied, "For awhile there I did not think you were going to talk to me."

"I was taken back," I replied. "You see I have somewhat of a problem and I do not know how to resolve it."

The form responded promptly to my statement, "I'm sure that I will be able to help you with that problem…in fact, I was sent here to do that very thing," the form assured me.

"First," the form insisted, "let me introduce myself."

"My name is Eric, and you may certainly call me by my name," the form graciously announced.

So, the form has a name, Eric to be exact! That was good to know. I could now speak to the form. I wondered then, if I had a name or if I was just a form like Eric.

"I am a male, just like you," Eric proclaimed.

Evidently Eric knew what was on my mind.

"We are not forms but beings," continued Eric. "Our forms are really bodies, created by the Almighty One. There are three types of beings, male, female, and angel spirit beings. We have names and identities by which we are known," he said with a most assuring tone of voice.

That was fine, but it really did not comfort me. I asked Eric, "What's my name and my identity…do you know?"

"Yes," replied Eric, "but for now I am not allowed to tell you."

"Why is that?" I queried him, but he only responded by saying, "be patient, in a short time you will know. But I can assure you that you are a male form."

I wondered what a short time meant. I wanted to know who I was. What my name was. What was my identity? Right away, I wanted to know! Eric was my only source of information. I did not want him to leave me so I became what he called patient. In fact, I didn't try to be patient; it came to me just naturally. This place, that I was in, appeared to have that type of an affect upon me. Eric seemed to be very patient also. The whole place had an air of patience.

The Almighty One, Who was that? What form was the Almighty One? There were more questions now for me to deal with. The situation was fast becoming rather complex.

"Eric," I asked. "Who is this Almighty One and what is the Almighty One's form?"

"Well, I can't give you a complete, nor even a satisfying, answer now. You will know more later about the Almighty One as you increase in your knowledge and understanding," responded Eric somewhat hesitantly.

"But this you can know. The Almighty One is a male form-not quite like us-and He is the One who makes all of this possible and sustainable. He has always been here, and always will be here."

Well, that was good to know. My curiosity was certainly aroused. Immediately I felt a great awe within me about this male form called the Almighty One. I was sure, for some reason unknown to me, that I would learn more about Him in the time ahead. From the way I felt, He must be very special.

I remembered then that Eric had said to me that he was here to help me. Perhaps the Almighty One had sent him. Quickly I asked Eric, "Did the Almighty One send you to help me?"

"No," said Eric, quite emphatically.

"The Archangel sent me. He has those types of responsibilities. He is one of the Almighty One's choice captains."

"What about this place? What is it?" I blurted out to Eric. "Have you always been here too?" I continued to question him.

I needed some answers, and soon. My mind was racing from one thought to another. It was strange. I should have been frustrated, but somehow I felt an assurance that all would be well. I was patient. An unexplainable calm flowed through me. A voice within me said, just wait; you will be receiving answers to your questions just when you need them.

"This place that you are in is paradise above," declared Eric, followed by that quiet smile of his. "It is found in the Heaven of the Heavenlies," he added.

His sudden response to my question jolted me out of my thoughts and back into the reality of my present situation.

Paradise, Heaven of the Heavenlies. I did not really understand this, but somehow I knew that Paradise was a special place. That was certainly obvious. Just looking around this place and being in this atmosphere was evidence of that. Heaven of the Heavenlies…that was different. I sure did not understand that. I am in Paradise Above and this Paradise is in the Heaven of the Heavenlies. Perhaps again, I thought, it will all become clearer in the times ahead. But for now, it remained mostly a great mystery.

Eric continued to speak to me. "I have been here on many occasions throughout the ages, but I have also been away, many times, performing specific assignments," he shared with me. "Now, though, you are my specific assignment. That is why I am here, to be of assistance to you through this process that you are now experiencing, and which you will continue to go through. When you have completed this process, then, you will no longer have need of me," he confidently informed me.

"I'm sure that we will get along," he added.

"I'm looking forward to our association with one another." While speaking, he reached out his hand to me and automatically I grasped his hand with mine, and we shook them in an up and down motion. Somehow that seemed to settle it. We would be friends. With that I knew Eric would not only be a helper, but a friend.

"It's time to move on," announced Eric, "we need to go to your place."

"What place?" I questioned. "Do I have a place; what about this place?" I was confused. Was I not in a place? This place that Eric said was Paradise Above.

"Eric," I said, "you told me I was in this place, Paradise Above. Do you mean there is another place?"

"Yes, there is," he stated. "You see, Paradise Above is very, very large. It covers a whole lot of space in the Heaven of Heavenlies. Within it are numerous other places; and you have one especially prepared for you."

"Eric, do you mean that this place was prepared for me," I asked him, being somewhat puzzled.

"Yes, just for you," Eric responded.

"But, then you knew I would be here before I arrived!" I replied.

"Yes, that is correct; the Almighty One knows everything, even before it happens," stated Eric, as if that was something that I should know or that it was general knowledge.

"Let's move on, we need to leave now," urged Eric. "Just come along with me and I will show you your prepared place."

I had no other choice but to go with Eric. After all, it would be an adventure. It would be another learning time. I sure had a lot to learn. There were so many unknowns. Just think, I had a place prepared for me. Was I special or something? What was this place like?

"Are you coming?" asked Eric.

He had already gone ahead of me walking on what appeared to be a path though a group of bright green towering trees.

"Yes," I shouted as I ran to catch up with him.

CHAPTER 2

Paradise Above

I wasn't sure what Paradise Above was. It was completely beautiful. Could one even imagine a more stunning place? I could not!

As Eric and I walked down this brightly-lit path, I stopped and looked upon all that was about me. Everything I gazed upon had a golden like glow emanating from it. Everywhere the glow was evident. The perfumed air permeated my nostrils with its scented fragrance. The tranquility of the place continued to give me a feeling of complete serenity.

"We have not arrived at your place yet," remarked Eric, as he nudged me on my shoulder. "We need to keep moving on, or we will never get there."

"There's so much to see," I retorted. "If we don't stop, I'll miss all of this beauty," I insisted.

"All of Paradise Above is like this, and even more. You will have plenty of time to see and enjoy all that the Almighty One has created," he assured me.

I believed what Eric said. It was so tempting though to stop occasionally to observe the abundance of beauty that surrounded me. Eric was patient with me. After all, he was my guide and my friend. I needed to cooperate with him. I certainly was dependent upon him.

Yet, the desire to stop here and there to see what the Almighty One had done was difficult to suppress.

"All right, Eric," I said, rather begrudgingly as I turned on the path toward where he was waiting. "I'll try not to stop anymore." Hopefully, I can do this, I thought.

We continued down the pathway through towering trees. I could see patches of brilliant blue skies above me as we walked along. I wanted to stop and look, to take all this beauty into my being without being hurried. Those trees were majestic. They stood tall, raising their brilliant, green leafy branches reaching upward into the blue above. Eric and I were both dwarfed by them. Yet, there appeared to be no shade from the trees, except for a few places where large bushes of dark red flowers grew. Even in this forest of great trees the light, with that golden like glow, was everywhere. Is this light from the Almighty One, I wondered? Is this light a reminder that His presence is everywhere?

Eric continued to lead the way. "When will we arrive at my place?" I thought. Yet, this walk had been so enjoyable, so pleasant, that I was not at all concerned about arriving at our destination soon…where ever that may be.

As we traveled along the path, I couldn't help but notice that we would enter into areas where there were no trees at all. These areas were great open spaces, covered with lush green grass-grass as high as my knees. The grass would move all in one direction, first one way and then another way. A fragrant, gentle breeze blew through these great open spaces.

Somehow, for some unexplainable reason unknown to me, I was able to think and talk about all that I had seen. I understood Eric when we exchanged our verbal communication. I was able to identify things that were all around me. I could even describe the breeze I saw flowing upon the grass as we journeyed through those expansive, open spaces. I have no recollection of ever learning how to speak, or for that matter, ever developing any type of thought patterns. Yet, I was functioning in all of these areas, and feeling quite confident in utilizing this ability. At this time, it seemed that the only plausible explanation to this mystery was that the Almighty One had something to do with it. When the occasion arrives, I must ask Eric. Certainly, he should know. But if he does know, will he share that with me?

"You know you are lagging behind?" I heard Eric asking me. Sure enough, he was way out in front of me.

It had been extremely difficult for me to resist the urge to stop and look around, but I kept going as I promised Eric. Nevertheless, I could see that my pace had slowed down considerably, and that I was lagging behind Eric.

"Wait up, Eric," I yelled to him. "I'm sorry that I got behind. I did not stop, but everything is so new and so breath-taking that I must have slowed my walk without noticing it." I attempted to explain to him as I reached the spot where he was waiting on the path.

"I understand your astonishment and your desire to see all of this unsurpassed beauty," Eric said sympathetically. "Remember, I told you that you will have time to see and even to explore some of this on your own?"

"Yes, I do," I answered.

"Well then," Eric continued, "be patient, and just be patient that time will come soon."

"How soon?" I replied, even though at this time I had very little understanding of what time, in essence, was.

Eric looked at me, he reached out and put his hand on my shoulder and looked into my eyes. We stood there face to face. Then with an expression of understanding upon his face, he said to me, "I want you to be assured that I am your friend. I've been sent to be your guide. I have only your best interest at heart."

I knew that. I trusted him. I did believe he was a friend sent to help me. I was glad that he again confirmed that to me. Still, I did not know who I was, or why I was here in the Paradise Above. Though I must admit, I have learned a few things. I know about Paradise Above, and most of all I know something about the Almighty One. Well, I thought, I'm even learning about Eric. It appears that he may be one of those angel beings. I'll have to ask him about that. It will be interesting to hear how he responds to my question.

"Thank you, Eric. I know you are my friend and my guide. I do trust you," I earnestly replied. Then as an afterthought I said, "You are the only one, Eric, that I have to rely upon for guidance. I want you to know that I appreciate you and your efforts to assist me."

Eric seemed very pleased to hear that, but he reminded me of our task to journey to my special place. "I appreciate you also," he said. "But we must continue, for we have some time to make up," he spoke emphatically.

With all of that said, Eric turned and led us down the path through another stand of towering trees. I followed behind obediently.

Some of the places that we traveled through had small ponds that were fed by streams of sparkling clear water. I had noticed them along the way, but I did not give them much attention. Most of those ponds had various-sized colorful rocks around them, forming somewhat of a border. Many of the streams feeding these ponds flowed over rocks. They created miniature rainbows as the waters tumbled over the colored rocks and fell into the ponds waiting below. To my eyes it was a dazzling display of multicolored brilliance.

Now that I was paying more attention to these streams and ponds, they appeared to be everywhere. In fact, as I observed closely, there was a fast-moving stream just parallel to the path upon which Eric and I were traveling. Funny, I had not really noticed that stream before. Yet, it had been there all of the time. I stopped, as if automatically, and looked toward Eric who was continuing on the path ahead.

"Eric, can you wait a minute?" I pleaded. "I want to ask you one quick question. It won't take long," I promised. "All these streams and all these ponds of water, where did they come from, and what are they for?" I blurted out.

Eric stopped, turned toward me, and walked back where I was standing and gazing into the stream next to our path. "I hope this will be our last interruption before we arrive at your place," Eric replied in somewhat of a commanding voice. "We are almost to your place," he continued, "and once we arrive, there will be time to talk about all you have seen. But for now, let this suffice for you," he said with a hopeful inflection in his voice. "The water that goes in these streams and ponds is what sustains the life and beauty of all that grows in Paradise Above. The water flows from the River of Life, which flows from the throne of the Almighty One. Without this water, Paradise Above would not be Paradise."

"Thank you for taking the time to tell me this," I said, gratefully. "But will I be able to see this River of Life myself?"

"In due time," replied Eric. "Now let's continue on our journey. As I said before, we are nearly there. Let's not have any more delays," he added, somewhat hurriedly.

So we were off again toward my place. Eric must have been disappointed with our previous pace, for it seemed that we were walking faster now. He appeared determined to make up for lost time. This fast pace didn't slow my thoughts. In fact, it seemed to accelerate them. My mind was full of what I had already experienced, and at the same time questions kept coming to my mind. What about all that I've seen in Paradise Above, and what about the Almighty One? What is my place like? What am I going to do there? Most of all, who am I?

Just then, when I was collecting my thoughts and organizing all my questions that needed answers, Eric suddenly stopped. I almost bumped into him, because he stopped so abruptly.

"Is there something wrong, Eric?" I asked him. "Why are we stopping, I thought you were in a hurry?"

"We are stopping because we are really behind our schedule," he responded, "and I need to change our mode of travel. At this pace we definitely will be too late!"

"Eric, what do you mean, change our mode of travel?" I questioned him. "Is there another way to travel?"

Eric's face beamed with a wide smile. "Yes, there is," he answered, "but we are not to use it unless there is a special occasion." He continued to smile at me as he answered. It was as if he was enjoying something while talking about it before it actually happened. I certainly did not know what he meant. Nor, did I see or feel any delight about stopping as we did and talking about a change in our travel. The stop, though, was good because I could now again observe all that was about me without feeling rushed.

Eric looked at me, quite earnestly and said, "What we are about to do will be different than what we have done. We can do this together, as long as you are with me. You cannot do this by yourself. I have this capability within myself alone."

What was he talking about? I could not understand him. He could do something I could not do, but with him I could do what he can do. I was confused. Eric then held out his arms, that is, he extended them out from his side in the air. Then he gave me some strange instructions. "Stand behind me, and put your arms about my waist, and hold on tightly. We are about to change our mode of travel," he instructed me with his still-smiling face. I did what Eric asked. I was a bit reluctant, but I trusted him. I stood behind him and grasped my hands around his waist. Then, I wondered, what's next?

"Hold on tight now, and whatever you do, do not let go." Eric sternly commanded me.

"All right, Eric." I assured him.

"Okay," Eric warned, "here we go!"

Before I knew what had happened, we instantly left the path that we were standing on and ascended straight up through the trees towards the blue space above. It was so sudden. My feet were not on the path anymore, even though my legs were still walking.

"You can stop walking now," Eric told me, "You are flying, not walking, so just let your legs trail behind you and enjoy the trip."

We were above the trees, soaring over the open grass spaces… over the streams and ponds. What a wonderful way to travel. As I looked down, I could see so much that I had not seen from the pathway that we traveled just a while ago. The beauty of it all was there. That had not changed, but my perspective did. This most definitely was a superior mode of travel! Now I knew why Eric was smiling. I found myself smiling also. What an adventure! Flying was a delightful mode of travel.

I continued to survey everything as we flew. I noticed a side river of water with multiple streams flowing from it to a myriad of sparkling ponds throughout the landscape below. It must be the River of Life. I could its flow to the very source. It was from that place with that golden glowing light. That was the brightest Place I have ever seen. I thought it must be the Place of the Throne of the Almighty One. Looking ahead and just above us, I saw two very bright spots. Those were curious things to me, and I wondered what they were.

Eric seemed to know what I was thinking. "Those are the sun and the moon," he explained, "they provide light both day and night for those below. We don't need them here in Paradise Above. The light from the Almighty One is greater than those. His light is all we need here."

I did not say anything more to Eric. I tried not to think about any more questions, or seek any more answers. Well, not just now. I already had more new things to deal with: sun, moon, day, night, those below, and this wonderful mode of flight. I was not going to give Eric more opportunities to inform me of more new things. I was becoming overwhelmed with all of these experiences. I needed a recess or a break just to process and assimilate all that has occurred.

We were descending now, rapidly approaching the trees below. The path that we had been on came into view. The stream beside it was still flowing with water. We went down through the trees as easily as we had earlier ascended through them.

The next thing I knew I was standing on that familiar path with Eric. His arms came down to his side. "You can let go now," Eric said. "We are at your place. Just follow me down this side path." There was excitement in his voice as he led me along this smaller path. I followed him. I was excited also. I was coming to my place-my special place. Before I knew it we stopped at a spot next to the path. There was an opening in the trees, like a doorway. Eric walked in and I followed.

"We are here, at your place," Eric exclaimed.

CHAPTER THREE

Special Place

Here I am in my special place. It had been an exhilarating journey for me. I thought now that I'm here; I need to look this place over thoroughly. This place was like many that I had recently seen. It was a great open space covered with a field of vibrant green grass, forming a border of this magnificently-lush space were spiraling trees shaped like a triangle. Just below the trees were flowering bushes of all imaginable colors, emitting the most pleasurable scents that one could inhale.

Gorgeous beds of flowers were scattered throughout the open space. They were raised in mounds of red-like soil. Crystal clear streaming water meandered through the grassy space, flowing in and out of numerous sparkling ponds. As I noticed previously in other spaces, the ponds were bordered with rocks that allowed for small waterfalls from the incoming streams.

I did not realize it at the time, but Eric was watching me closely as I viewed my special place. He had a most curious look upon his face. He seemed very interested in how I was responding to my introduction into my special place. Actually, I was speechless completely mesmerized by the overwhelming beauty of this amazing place.

"Well," Eric queried, "What do you think?"

I barely heard his question. I was still in a state of awe. I could hardly believe that this was my place.

"Did you not hear me?" Eric asked again in a louder voice. This time I heard him clearly. "I'm sorry Eric," I replied, "everything in this space is so wonderful that for a moment I was hypnotized by all that I was seeing."

Eric appeared to be impressed by my excitement.

"Eric, thank you for bringing me here. I think it's absolutely wonderful!" I was truly grateful to him, and extremely pleased with my special place. I wanted him to know that. Upon hearing my response to his question, Eric's face beamed with a radiant smile-a smile that I'd learned to appreciate fully in our brief time together.

"I'm so glad you like it. It will be your home for a while until you finish your process." Eric declared.

"What process?" I asked.

Eric looked puzzled. "Don't you recall that I mentioned this to you-that there are things you needed to know and to do while you are here?" Eric responded to my question with one of his own. I remembered now that we had talked about this just after we had first met. Eric said, as I recall, that he was sent to be my assistant as I went through the process of knowing about being here in Paradise Above and learning of the Almighty One.

"Yes, Eric I remember now," I apologized.

"Fine, now let's walk over there to the section of your place where you can rest, study, meditate, and we can sit down to discuss your process," Eric said as he nudged me in that direction. "That's better than just standing here," he explained.

I did not have time to think about what Eric had just said, or even to question him. He moved off to a corner of my space and I quickly followed. I was eager to discuss with him this 'process'. We approached a smaller group of trees, which I had not before noticed. They blended so much into the landscape of the bordering trees, that I could easily have overlooked them. Apparently this was the case. As we drew nearer to this stand of trees, they appeared smaller than the trees lining the border of the space. Among the trees', bright, yellow-green leaves were various colored objects suspended from their branches. Another pond was in the midst of the trees. There were a number of white objects surrounding the pond, and a few were located under some nearby trees.

More things to learn, I thought to myself. Surely Eric will explain to me what this part of my special space is, and how it relates to me.

"This is probably the one place in your space where you will spend a considerable amount of your time," Eric announced, smiling. Eric evidently had some idea of what I was thinking, for he began to inform me about this place.

"These white objects are for your comfort. They are also helpful for your study time and meditation periods," he continued. "These are chairs for sitting." I looked as he pointed to them. "There is a lounge for resting, and some tables for your convenience." He pointed to them as he kept talking. "You can move them around and arrange them as you like. I suggest that you keep them in this area of your space for efficiency sake," he added.

"Excuse me for carrying on so hurriedly," Eric apologized, while he kept talking. "I just want you to feel at home, and now that we are here, in your special place, there is so much more that I want to share with you. But in order to do that it was necessary that we first arrive here."

Well, that statement really aroused my interest. I was ready to have more information. Now, perhaps, I would find out who I was and what I was doing here.

"Sit down here," Eric requested, as he pulled a chair to where I was standing. I sat down. The chair was sturdy and comfortable. I realized this was the first time that I sat down since I got here. It was very enjoyable. Eric pulled up a chair near me, and sat down. We were now facing each other.

Eric looked at me intently. Slowly and quietly he said, "Please do not interrupt me until I've finished talking to you. Then I will answer your questions, or as much as I can, or am allowed. Will you promise to do that?" he asked.

I had no other choice. Could I refrain from asking questions while he was talking? I was sure I could. I had been holding questions back for quite a while anyway. So this promise should be easy for me to honor. I looked at Eric with an assuring smile and said, "I will."

"First of all, I want you to stand up and walk over to the pond right behind you," Eric commanded. "When you arrive at the edge, look into the water and tell me what you see."

Why does he want me to do that? I wondered why he told me to sit down, and then almost immediately after I sat down, he asked me to stand and walk to the pond. Nevertheless, it was important for me to cooperate with Eric. I wanted to know so much. I felt that this must be one of the steps I needed to take to attain the knowledge I wanted. I got up and approached the pond. I stopped at the edge, and peered into the sparkling clear water. I could see sand and rocks strewn on the bottom of the pond. But, also, I saw an image in the water. It was a form, or rather a body, as Eric had informed me earlier. The body in the water appeared to be identical to Eric's body, with one notable exception. The body image shimmering in the water was dressed in a bright, red robe that extended down to within a few inches from the ground. The robe had a wide, white sash. It was tied around the waist so as to keep it fitted to the body.

"Well, what do you see?" questioned Eric. "Are you speechless?"

I heard Eric speaking to me. He seemed far off. I could only stand there at the water's edge and gaze into the pool. I could not take my eyes off the figure mirrored there. I was transfixed. Was that me? That image in the water? I decided to move my arms to see if the image would do the same thing, so while still looking into the water I raised both my arms over my head. Sure enough, the image in the water did so too. Then, I walked around the pond to see if I could leave the image. But, no matter which way I went, or what actions I made with my body, the image performed the same things. There was no denying it that must, somehow, be my image. But wait. I know…I'll put my hand into the watered image to see if it's really me. I bent down on one knee and extended my hand into the water. The water was cool, and as my hand dipped into the pond a series of ripples formed and flowed to the water's edge. But in those ripples, I saw a face looking up at me. Instantly, I knew that was my face. I was face to face with my face!

"Can you not answer me?" Eric called with a louder voice. "I'm waiting to hear from you."

"Just a moment, Eric, just a moment," I pleaded. "I can't talk to you just now." I replied.

"Okay," Eric said in a resigned voice, "but do hurry, won't you?"

That was my face. It looked young, like Eric's face. The eyes were brown and set wide apart from the nose. Brown eyebrows and black eyelashes gave the eyes an expression of depth and vitality. The nose was moderately large and straight. Full lips graced a chiseled jaw. When the face smiled, it exposed perfectly-formed white teeth. The face and head were almost like Eric's, but Eric had golden-colored hair on his head and blonde eyebrows. His face was more of a white complexion, while my face was darker and ruddy. My hair was brownish black. What I saw in the water pond was the image of me. That's what I looked like. I stood up. I liked what I saw.

I walked rapidly back to where Eric was sitting. Needless to say, I was extremely excited. I knew what I looked like. Did I have a name or some type of identity? What am I doing here? Where did I come from? Now, at least, I believed I would have my questions answered finally.

Eric stood up as I approached him. He was smiling as he asked, "What did you see? Tell me."

"I saw myself," I replied happily. "Now I know what I look like. In fact, I look somewhat like you, with the exception of our hair and eye color, facial complexion, and the color of our robes. Why these differences?" I inquired.

"Remember our earlier conversation?" Eric asked. He continued to talk as if he had already received an answer from me. "I told you there were three types of beings, apart from the Almighty One. There exists male, female, and spirit angel beings. We have bodies but they, at times, are not exactly the same. Your body is a male tabernacle body prepared for you by the Almighty One for the time that you are here in Paradise Above. Angels are robed in white. Tabernacle male and female beings are robed in red. My body is not the same as your body, although our bodies appear to be the same. There are special abilities that I have with my male angel body that you do not posses.

For instance, you can raise your arms and hands as if to fly but you will be incapable of leaving the ground. But, as you have already experienced, I have this capability-the ability to leave the ground and to soar over the trees in the blue above." Eric paused as if to catch his breath.

"Go on Eric, don't stop now," I insisted. I was receiving more information, and I certainly did not want Eric to stop sharing that information with me.

"Let's see, where did I leave off?" Eric asked.

"You were talking about our bodies Eric-about flying and all that," I reminded him.

"Oh, yes," Eric continued. "I'm a spirit angel being, created by the Almighty One for service to Him and to others. You are a male being in a tabernacle body created by the Almighty One. You are here in Paradise Above in the Heaven of Heavenlies for a purpose. That purpose will be revealed to you as you go through the process."

"Wait a minute Eric, please slow down," I requested as I abruptly interrupted him.

"I understand about the bodies now, and their differences. But this purpose and process thing-explain this slowly to me, Eric, so I am able to understand it without you repeating yourself too much," I requested somewhat hesitantly.

"All right, but listen carefully. Please do not interrupt me again. Remember you promised," Eric readily reminded me. "You are here to learn about yourself, Paradise Above, and most of all, about the Almighty One. While you are here, you will have the assignment to maintain this space, this special space of yours. You need to be sure that the flowers and those trees with those multicolored fruit are well watered. You are to make sure that the streams are kept open and clear to feed the flowers and trees. By the way, the water is available for drinking, and the fruit is food for you to eat. Both the water and the fruit are delicious and quite refreshing. You will notice that there are cups, dishes, and silverware on shelves just below the table tops for your use. You will find gardening tools in that upright cabinet over there next to the clump of trees." Eric pointed to all of these areas where those things were located, and I was careful to take note of where they were.

"Here in Paradise Above, we all speak and understand the Heavenly language. I know you are saying to yourself that you have no recollection of ever learning to speak a language, let alone understanding the language. That special ability is automatically given to anyone who comes here, including you. You will be able to continue in the process in a more rapid way as you start your first session tomorrow. I will have to leave you now, but if you need me just think about me and call me in your mind. I will get the message and come immediately. So just make yourself at home. Do some gardening, eat, drink, and get some rest. I'll come a little later to take you to your first session. You won't be alone. There will be others like you there. Meanwhile, stay here in your space," Eric concluded.

Eric started to raise his arms over his head. I could see he was getting ready to fly.

"Wait, Eric," I yelled, "you said I could ask questions if I didn't interrupt you. You told me," I continued, "to be patient and my questions would be answered."

"They will be," Eric shouted back as he hung over my space just above the colored fruit trees. "Just give it some time," he assured me. "We will start on some of them later when I pick you up for your first session." Eric began to fly higher above my space. I looked up and followed his ascent as he rose to the top of the tall trees bordering my space. Then he stopped, momentarily looked down at me and said, "I almost forgot to tell you this. I don't know what your name is or what it will be, but you do have a number, that is, for now. Your identity number is 155. So we will just call you One Fifty-Five."

With that announcement made, Eric disappeared from my view, and left me staring into the limitless blue above my space.

CHAPTER FOUR

Revelation

So, my identity number is 155. Eric said that he'd call me One Fifty-Five. I'm a number. I don't have a name. He did say that he did not know my name, and even if I was given a name he would not know what it would be. I was happy though. This was a promising start. I was someone with identity-a recognizable being. That fact, in and of itself, was most reassuring.

I had a place to myself. An extremely beautiful space to care for, and most of all to enjoy thoroughly. I felt vibrant, alive and robust. It was enough now, just sitting here in my lounge, thinking about my identity number 155. But, I need to get up and personally survey this special space of mine, to examine all the streams that were flowing from the ponds to the flowers and fruit trees. To see if they were free of grass or rocks that would impeded the waters flow. Everything looked in order, though I did pick up a few rocks that had fallen into the stream, and deposited them on the pond's border.

I inspected the fruit trees. Each tree, with its own brightly-colored fruit, was most alluring. I was not sure which one I should taste first. Didn't Eric say that the fruit was there to eat? That the fruit was my food-delicious to the taste. The red fruit was especially appealing. It was the size of both my clasped hands, and a bit larger. I reached up to the big red fruit just above my head and plucked it from its branch. I gazed at it in my hands, lifted it to my mouth, and tasted my first bite of the fruit from the trees of Paradise Above. That bite is one that I shall never forget. As soon as I bit into the fruit, a juicy flavor of vanilla-like sweetness invaded my taste buds. Then, as I swallowed that piece of fruit, the sweetness emanated throughout my entire being. The smell of the fruit filled the air around me and penetrated my nostrils with every breath. I proceeded quickly to devour this tasty fruit. Eating fruit, just as Eric said, was not only a delicious experience, but an exhilarating one. Did I have to eat this fruit periodically or regularly to sustain me? I wondered about that. I'll ask Eric when he comes. But for now I will just try a few more fruits.

Hurriedly I went from one tree to another, eating and tasting the different-colored fruits. To my surprise each fruit had a different taste, with its own unique flavoring and scent. With every bite of each fruit, my eating and smelling experience was the same as when I first ate the red fruit. I noticed that no matter how many fruits I consumed, I never felt really full. The flavor and the scent of the fruit remained delicious and exhilarating, but there seemed to be no material substance to the fruit itself. I thought that to be strange, but I didn't care to pursue the matter, and consequently dismissed it from my mind. Without thinking anymore, I returned to my lounge area, picked up a glass from beneath the table, and scooped some water out of the nearby stream. As if it were natural for me, I drank all the water without stopping. It was refreshingly cool and bubbly. The water was revitalizing, even energizing. Drinking it heightened my awareness of those things around me. I sat down, looked around, and began to reflect on all that had happened. Then, it occurred to me that it was a privilege to be here.

"Did you enjoy the fruit?" sounded a voice just behind me.

"Yes, I surely did," I replied, recognizing Eric's voice as I turned my head to locate him. It was Eric, just as I thought.

"I heard you thinking of me One Fifty-Five, and thought I'd drop in for a little chat."

"I don't remember calling you Eric," I responded in a puzzled voice. "Why are you here?"

Eric smiled. Then he approached me and sat down on the chair next to my lounge. Again we were face to face.

"Remember when you were eating the fruit and wondering if you needed to eat this fruit to remain alive or to sustain yourself?" he asked.

"Now that you mention it, I remember that thought. Oh now I remember, I wanted to ask you about that also." I responded to Eric, completely amazed.

"Eric, how did you know?"

"Well, One Fifty-Five," Eric proceeded to explain, "I told you earlier that if you think of me that I would be available to come to your aid. One of my main responsibilities is to be of assistance to you while you are here in Paradise Above. So, here I am, eager to help."

There was no doubting his sincerity. I could tell by his beaming face and the tone of his voice that he took pleasure in being here with me-that he truly desired to help me. I felt special and honored to have Eric, not only as a friend, but as my guide. Suddenly Eric interrupted my thought saying, "you do not need the fruit to sustain you. It is for your pleasure. Your tabernacle body is self-sustaining as long as you occasionally drink the waters of the River of Life which flows from the Throne of the Almighty One. That water is in all the ponds and streams in Paradise Above. Probably, though, you will prefer to drink the water quite often, for it is joyously refreshing, energizing, and highly tasteful. It is the Almighty One's gift to all that dwell in Paradise Above."

Eric kept talking. He was full of information and knowledge, which I now knew, was of vital importance to me. There were so many questions to ask him. If I interrupted him, I would miss out on what he was now revealing to me. So, I just listened to him, absorbing all that he shared with me. There would be times, I was sure, during his pauses, that I would be able to slip in a few questions during this one-sided conversation.

Eric continued. I listened intently. "This water never dissipates. It is always here. The flow stays the same. Those fruit you picked and ate from the trees-look at the branches of the trees where you obtained the fruit. What do you see One Fifty-Five?" Eric said, pointing to the trees in a challenging way.

I looked at those trees and their branches from where I picked the fruit, and surprisingly new fruit had grown there. "Eric!" I exclaimed. "It's as if the fruit was never picked!"

Eric assured me that fresh, delicious fruit would always be available for my eating pleasure.

"Do you eat this fruit also, Eric, and drink this water?" I inquired.

"Yes, I do on occasion, but we angel beings also have special food for our pleasure which is provided by the Almighty One. This food is not necessarily available to tabernacle beings," he explained.

"What does it taste like?" I was inquisitive. "Is it like this fruit with its flavor and scent?"

"Not exactly," he replied, "it's more of a honey, syrupy taste, nor is it shaped like a fruit. It is more like a wafer shape, small and round, somewhat flat, indented with random perforations. The people down below, at one time, ate this food. They called it manna."

"The people down below, Eric, are they like me?" I asked.

"You mention that often. I mean, you refer to down below and to Paradise Above. Should I know about this? Are there male and female beings there also? Do they have angel beings like you to assist them?" The questions kept tumbling out of my mouth as I rapidly presented them to Eric. I didn't even give him time to answer one question before inquiring with another.

Eric nodded his head with every question, as if he was cataloging each one of them to be answered.

"Wait a minute," Eric said, holding up his hand towards me. "One Fifty Five, you are filled with questions, and I can't answer all of them at once for your satisfaction. I'll have to take them one at a time," he calmly told me.

Eric continued. "Even the answers I share with you will not completely answer your questions. Some of these questions will be more fully answered at the coming sessions you will be attending. This is all part of your process."

"All right Eric, I'm all ears, I'll hold off on any more questions, well, for now," I promised him. This was getting extremely interesting. I eagerly waited for Eric to answer these questions. Eric said nothing. He dropped his hand, put it on his lap, closed his eyes, and lowered his head. I wondered if something was wrong with him.

"Eric, are you all right, are you going to talk to me?" I asked him nervously.

Still Eric said nothing. I was immediately concerned. Maybe he is not going to answer me at all. I have never seen Eric act like this before. He seemed strange to me.

"I'm sorry One Fifty- Five." That startled me as he unexpectedly looked up and began to speak. "I was just thinking how I could answer you. Yes, I'm all right. Again excuse me for the delay in my answer and for being silent." Eric graciously replied.

I felt better now. Eric seemed to be his usual self. "Well," I urged him, "tell me about these things."

"Down below is a place called earth," Eric slowly began to expound. He appeared very somber as his usual smile vanished from his face. I could tell by the way he began to speak that this was going to be a lengthy explanation. So, I lay back in the lounge chair and gave him my full attention. I did not want to miss anything that he was going to say.

"As I was saying," Eric reiterated, "down below is a place called Earth. They have days and nights and years that they refer to as time. Here in Paradise Above, it is different as we do not have these things. Beings live on earth, both male and female. They produce other male and female beings as they marry. They join their bodies together in a certain way, and a short time later the female being becomes pregnant. That is, she is now carrying in her body a developing baby being. The baby being is the product of the female's seed that she has within her body, being united with the male's seed. When the two seeds meet, the baby begins to form within the female. The baby is alive and growing within her body, and when the baby, whether it is female or male being, is fully formed, that baby will leave the female mother and be born. Then the baby is independent from the mother, and is free to grow into an adult being. The pregnancy stage lasts nine months, according to Earth's time, for the baby to be born. Growing to an adult stage after birth, generally takes about twenty years. Most beings on Earth live about seventy to eighty years after birth before they die." Eric stopped to catch his breath.

I was glad he did. I needed to think about those things he had just related to me. "Eric," I thought aloud, "do we do that here in Paradise Above-that is marry and have babies?"

Eric smiled, broke into laughter, and looked at me. I could see a twinkle in his eyes as his laughter gradually subsided to a glowing smile.

"Forgive my laughter," he implored, "but what you asked was funny. I could not help but laugh-not at you, but at your question. Of course, you have no idea about these things, and you just proceeded to ask a very natural question." Eric looked at me sympathetically and continued to talk. "Down below those people have natural bodies which eventually die. Up here all the male and female beings have tabernacle bodies. They do not marry and have babies. Also they do not die."

I sat up from the lounge abruptly. "Eric," I exclaimed, "was I ever on Earth? Did I have a natural body and die?" I was excited! All kinds of thoughts flooded my mind as I blurted out these questions.

Eric looked at me. He appeared to grow very serious. When I asked those questions, I noticed a complete change of expression upon his face.

"Sit back on your lounge chair One Fifty-Five," speaking slowly and forcibly, he quietly instructed me.

As I did his bidding, I felt that something important was about to happen. I wasn't sure what it was, but somehow I experienced a feeling that something profound was going to take place.

I looked again at Eric. I could see that he sensed what I was feeling.

"I knew the time would come when we would arrive at this subject," Eric sighed. "Yes, at one time you were on Earth. There a male and a female united together; but they were not married. They engaged in the process of developing a baby. The female became pregnant, and within her body the baby was alive and growing.

Then, for various reasons, a decision was made to prevent the baby from being born. Consequently, the baby, as he was developing his natural body within the female, was killed. This occurred while he was still inside the female's body. The dead baby was extracted from the 'would be' mother's body. He was never born to live on Earth."

Eric stopped talking. There was silence. Neither one of us said a thing. I could hear the water flowing in the ponds. Occasionally a gentle breeze blew by, but that seemed so far away-all of it. I was afraid to ask Eric the question that was slowly but decisively permeating my mind. If I asked him, did I really want an answer, and did I want it now?

"Eric," I ventured, "I suspect that the story you just related is about me. Is that correct?"

"Yes," hesitantly Eric responded. His face was sad, and I saw tears in his eyes. "It's about you. You were killed before you were ever born. I was there. I saw it all, but I did not have the authority to prevent it from occurring. But you will learn, One Fifty-Five, that all being life, once it is initiated, never really ceases to exist. It simply changes forms and destinations. The Almighty One has planned and designed all of this."

I was stunned to the point of being speechless. Here I was in Paradise Above, having been killed, unborn and dead, while on Earth. "How could this be?" I thought.

Eric again knew my very thoughts. Without waiting for a question from me, he began to answer them.

"Like you, One Fifty-Five, all babies that are killed below, before they are born, are immediately transported, not in their natural bodies, to live in Paradise Above in the Heaven of the Heavenlies. They are supernaturally transformed by the redeeming power of the Almighty One into adult male or female beings in tabernacle bodies, never to age, nor ever to experience death again. There are many like you here in Paradise Above. You will see many of them soon when we go to your first session. Up here, we angel spirit beings refer to all of you with the red robes, as Rubs."

Eric seemed to be greatly relieved, as if some great burden had been lifted from him.

I sat there in that lounge chair, staring out into the blue above. My thoughts were afar off. I tried to remember if it was at all possible to recall the time I was killed. It was just a blank. I only remember the time when I first realized I was here in Paradise Above. Nothing, I concluded was in my memory before that.

"Are you all right?" Eric asked as he touched me on the shoulder.

"What's that, Eric?" I responded as his touch reminded me of what he had recently unfolded to me.

"Are you all right?" he repeated.

"Yes, Eric, I'm all right. It's difficult to understand being killed before one is born, yet being alive after being assumed dead." I responded still puzzled by it all.

"One Fifty-Five, I'm sure you will understand it more and more as you attend the sessions throughout your process program," Eric assured me as he began to raise his arms over his head to fly.

"Are you leaving again Eric?" I quickly asked before he ascended.

"Yes," he replied, "but I'll be back soon to take you to your first session."

"Wait, don't go yet!" I shouted.

Eric put his arms down, and in a somewhat anxious voice said, "Well, what is it?"

"Tell me, Eric, before you leave, what does Rub mean? You never did explain that."

Eric raised his arms above his head again and left the ground ascending above the ponds and the fruit trees, but then he stopped and looked down at me. "One Fifty-Five," he shouted to me. "'Rub' means Redeemed Unborn Babies."

Then Eric disappeared into the blue, leaving me with that revelation to ponder.

CHAPTER 5

To The Session

So, that is what I am-a RUB-a Redeemed Unborn Baby. From what I learned from Eric, I am also a male being, matured in age in a tabernacled body, identified with the number One Fifty-Five, dressed in a red robe with a white sash, and I have a special garden place of my own to maintain and enjoy-all of this in Paradise Above.

I've certainly learned a lot since my first meeting with Eric. In fact, I wondered where I would be without Eric? Probably I would still be standing where I first met him. But that seemed so long ago. I'm so thankful that the Almighty One assigned Eric to be my helper. He has brought me so far on what he calls my process. I wondered, how much more do I have to learn? Immediately it occurred to me that I had not even attended my first session. Then, reality set in-obviously I had a way to go.

While those thoughts occupied my mind, I got up from my lounge, and went to pick some fruit. Perhaps some delicious fruit will be enjoyable to eat at this time. I could use a refreshing pause from all these complex thoughts. No sooner had I arrived at that tree with the bright yellow fruit, than from above me I heard the sound of a very familiar voice.

"Oh, there you are," yelled Eric. "At first I didn't see you in your lounge area, One Fifty- Five, and thought that you may have strayed out of your space." He explained.

"No, Eric, as you can see, I'm just getting some fruit to eat. Want to join me?" I asked invitingly.

"We don't have time to do that here. We need to depart for your first session," Eric replied rather hurriedly, as he descended to the ground a few feet from where I was standing. "Look, pick a fruit for yourself and one for me and we can eat them along the way," he suggested.

So, off we went through my space, eating our fruit. Eric led the way down a narrow path. I followed behind him. We went through the border of tall trees that surrounded my space, and soon we intersected onto a much broader trail, and turned to the right to follow it. What I saw, as we turned on to that trail, caused me to stop abruptly. I was not prepared for this. It was completely overwhelming, if not shocking. I blinked my eyes! Could this be true what I was viewing? I turned to Eric. He had stopped also with me.

"Just stay here for a moment to observe the sight. I told you that there were more Rubs." He reminded me.

More Rubs was an understatement! As far as I could see both in front of, and behind me there was a mass of beings in red robes accompanied by white robed angel beings. They were all moving in one direction along this broad trail toward the bright light ahead of us. How could anyone count the number of them? They were too numerous. It would be impossible. They were coming out of the smaller trails through the tall trees, just as Eric and I had done, and were turning onto the broader trail. "Did they all have a special place like me?" I quietly asked myself. Each one appears to have his own Eric, or whatever their name might be. Evidently, we were all going to the same place for the session.

"You're right on all accounts One Fifty-Five," Eric said as he nudged me on my shoulder. "We need to move on now," he urged.

I kept looking around as we fell in with the other Rubs and their angels walking toward the bright light before us.

"Eric you knew what I was thinking, didn't you?" I admirably declared.

Eric responded patiently letting my voice subside, "You know I have that capability, don't you?" he retorted.

"Yes," I had to admit that I did know, "but please excuse my outburst Eric. I'm sorry."

Eric smiled at me graciously and said, "That's okay, I understand. Like I said," he continued, "you were right about everything except one thing. Each Rub has his own special space similar to yours as well as their personal angel being. Everyone has a little bit of Eden here in Paradise Above. Most of them have identifying numbers like you. Many have been here longer than others, and some are recent arrivals like you. All of them, including you, are going to be attending their first session as part of their process program."

"Well, Eric," I interrupted, "what is the exception?"

"Some Rubs have names, but very few. You will find out more about this in the future," he assured me. "Also, you won't believe this One Fifty-Five," Eric flippantly offered, "but all the spirit angel beings are named Eric."

"How can they be distinguished from one another?" I asked.

"Well, obviously not by name, but each Rub recognizes his own Eric personally. That is true also for each Eric and his Rub." Eric explained.

I didn't want to pursue the matter any further. Somehow, I knew I wouldn't fully understand it, even if it was thoroughly explained to me. So, I decided just to accept it as Eric said, and not to be concerned about it anymore.

While we continued on our walk toward the place where the session would be held, I noticed that all the Eric's looked pretty much the same. Their faces glowed brightly and all of them had golden-colored hair and wore white robes. They were all identical in height. Even their body shapes appeared to be identical. They were marvelous looking angelic male beings!

The Rubs were not the same. Although we were robed in red, we were not identical in body forms. Some were taller than others. Their faces were not all the same color as mine. Some had faces with a white complexion and various colors of hair. I noticed a wide range of hair colors…red, black, white, blonde, and a variety of brownish-colored hair among them. Other faces, which were most of them, were colored darker from light-brown complexions to even black-just about all of them had black hair. A number of them had longer hair and their faces were not as ruddy as the others. They had a different look about them, a softer face with a more delicate skin complexion. "Hmm" I wondered, "these are a different type of Rubs."

"You're getting very perceptive in your observations One Fifty-Five," Eric volunteered as his statement interrupted my thoughts.

"How is that? I asked.

"Well," Eric replied, "you noticed the difference in the Rubs. Those Rubs you were scrutinizing are female beings in tabernacled bodies."

"Is that who they are?" I asked again.

Eric looked at me questionably and said, "Don't you remember? I told you there were three types of beings that the Almighty One created: a male being, a female being, and an angelic spirit being. The male being and the female being are both human beings, and though they are similar in most respects, there are some differences between them. They were created that way." Eric paused with a sigh, "Well, soon enough you'll find out more."

"Is that all Eric?" I inquired. "What about angelic beings. I remembered you told me about them."

"Well you do remember, then why should I continue to explain?" he asked impatiently.

I did not mean to annoy him. "I just wanted to reaffirm that for my benefit, Eric. Thank you for being patient with me."

Our conversation abruptly ceased. We had come to another trail which caused the ranks of Rubs ahead of us to slow down, almost to a point of stopping. They were making a turn to the left onto a broader trail which was twice the width of the one on which we were now traveling. As we approached the turn, I was mindful of the bright light shining just ahead and to the right of us. It shone brighter here. It was so bright that you had to squint your eyes just a bit in order to see. Eric and I made the turn onto the broader trail, and I opened my eyes fully as we were now heading away from the bright light in another direction. To my amazement, I could not help but notice a broad river running parallel to our trail. It was as clear as crystal. I looked into its depth and clearly saw a golden colored bottom upon which it flowed. The water appeared to be dancing and sparkling all at the same time. Yet, it flowed smoothly in the direction that we were walking. There was definitely a restful quality about it. I could feel it. It had an immediate effect upon me. My concern about going to the session quickly disappeared, and it was surprisingly replaced with an attitude of eager anticipation.

"That's the River of God, the Almighty One, which flows from his throne," Eric informed me.

He knew my thoughts, as usual, and answered my question before I could even ask it.

"The water energizes and sustains all that is in Paradise Above. It is not only restful to look upon, refreshing to drink, but it is the very water of life from God Himself to all those who will freely drink it." Eric said.

Eric was right. I had experienced the drinking of that water. How exhilarating it was. How refreshing it was to me, and to think that it is from God, and that it is always available.

Suddenly the caravan of Rubs came to an abrupt halt. There was complete silence, except for the musical sound coming from the flowing water of the nearby river. I turned to Eric and ask him, "Why this sudden slow down?"

Eric pointed with his hand over the Rubs ahead of us and in the same direction we were traveling and said, "Look up One Fifty-Five. Look up yonder."

Eric's voice had a commanding tone to it. There must have been something of great importance to see! I didn't hesitate. I did as he insisted. I looked up yonder. "What am I looking for Eric?" I asked. I did not see anything at all except the trees bordering the trail ahead to my left and the blue above.

"Keep looking up yonder," Eric encouraged me.

I kept gazing up out yonder toward the blue above. Then I saw it. Arising in the distance was a white-shaped object. It was large-so large that it towered over the trees. "I see it now!" I exclaimed. "What is it Eric?"

"That's the building we are traveling to for your sessions. Evidently those Rubs ahead of us have stopped to admire it before they go inside and have caused us to stop here. Wait until you get there. If you are amazed now, it is only a prelude to what you will soon see." Eric promised excitedly.

The caravan of Rubs started moving again. I could hardly keep my eyes off that enormous building. As we came nearer to the structure, I could see that it blocked out most of the blue above. The building was a brilliant color of white. From where I was standing, I could not see the end of the building on either side or the top!

As we approached it, to enter in, it became impossible to view it in its entirety. I had lost sight of the river. It probably was flowing on the other side of this giant edifice.

"By the way, Eric, does this building have a name? Is there a name for it?" I inquired.

"It is called the Celestial Academy," Eric stated.

"Sounds appropriate to me. I can't wait to get inside!" I responded. I was eager to enter the hall and was really excited. My feelings were calm and controlled but I was still excited at the prospect of entering into this special building.

Just ahead were rows of massive glass doors lining the outside of the hall. Quietly they opened as we approached.

We all filed inside. The hall was shaped like half of a circle. There were rows and rows of white colored seats with each row lower than the other. All the seats faced toward the front of the semi-circle where a large golden curtain hung suspended over a raised stage. The Rubs kept entering the hall and sitting in seats row by row accompanied by their Erics.

Eric and I sat down directly in the center of the hall and about halfway up from the stage area. The Rubs were still coming into the building, quietly filling the seats-seat by seat and row by row.

I turned to Eric and asked him, "What type of hall is this?"

"This is the amphitheater of the Heavenly Assembly Hall. Here is where most, if not all, of your sessions will be held."

I wondered how many sessions there would be, and if we would be seated in the same row and seat each session. I decided not to ask as it was merely a trivial thought. The next time I came to another session I'd find out. By now the last of the Rubs had occupied the upper rows and seats. An Eric in a white robe seated next to a Rub in a red robe throughout the entire assembly hall gave the appearance of a colored checkered spectrum. I wondered if there was some special significance to the panorama. Perhaps red and white had some special meaning that extended beyond their actual colors. Eric should know, but is this a good time to ask him?

"Eric," I ventured. But as I started to ask him the question the lights grew dim in the assembly hall. The massive doors began to close and quickly a hush fell over the audience. My question would have to wait. The session was about to begin.

CHAPTER 6

The First Session

The silence was almost unbearable. Not a sound was heard-not even a breathing sound-as if everyone present was holding their breath. The hall had a lingering golden glow barely visible to the eye. There appeared to be a special presence pervading the atmosphere around us as if some invisible thing or person was everywhere present but unseen. The fragrance that had become so familiar to me in my special place was so noticeable here. Its indescribable scent permeated every space of the massive assembly hall! Everyone was aware of this, I'm sure, for as I gazed around the room observing all those red robed rubs and their Erics, I could see that they were affected by the wonder of it all, even as I was.

The silence was broken. A great sound bellowed throughout the hall. Every one released their breaths at the same time with one orchestrated, voluminous sigh. All of this happened in just a few moments of time. I thought to myself, "what a way to begin my first session...unforgettable."

But now the hall was filled with talking, as the Rubs began to communicate with each one of their Erics as they all collectively directed their attention to the front of the massive assembly hall. I too looked to the front of the hall. I observed a large structure ascending from the floor. I turned to Eric. It appeared that he was transfixed by it all, for he did not respond when I asked him.

"Eric, what is that?"

Finally Eric noticed me. "Did you say something 155?" he queried somewhat half heartedly, looking to me and then back to the rising structure.

I had never seen Eric like this before. It was as if he was not fully functioning. He always knew what was going on and appeared always to be in complete control. What was it, I wondered?

Just then the large black structure stopped its ascent and stood above the floor. A smaller structure then ascended from the larger one although it was much smaller with a broader plate on top of it. It too stopped rising somewhat above the larger structure.

"Eric," I asked as I nudged him, somewhat like he usually nudged me, "Do you know what all of this is?"

Eric smiled graciously. He seemed to be his usual self. "That big structure, the big black one, is a stage and the smaller structure is a podium," he precisely explained. "They are raised up like that so all in the hall will be able to see what will be happening there." He added. "By the way 155, you caught me by surprise a while ago when I was concentrating on all that was happening in the Assembly Hall. You see, this is the first time that I have been here also. This is my first session."

"Are you sure Eric?" I was dumbfounded and almost skeptical. "You're not just joking with me?" I pleaded.

"No, I'm not joking, not at all," he replied.

I could see he was serious. Any doubt I had quickly disappeared. "But Eric," I ventured, "don't you know what these sessions are all about? They are not for you, are they?"

"Yes, I know what they are all about, as you said, and yes, they are not for me but for you," he said with a reassuring look upon his face. "This is the first time I have been here and it is my first session. I would not have been here except for you," he said emphatically as he looked deeply into my eyes.

I could see in them a hint of sadness, not only in his eyes but also in the tone of his voice. "How is that so Eric?" I asked. I was puzzled. Had I forgotten something? Perhaps I did not understand.

"Earlier we mentioned this, but not completely," he offered almost apologetically. "Remember I've been with you from the beginning. I was and I still am assigned to you. I'm your guardian angel," he finished proudly.

"You are assigned to me Eric? You are my guardian angel?" I asked.

"Yes, that is true," answered Eric.

"But how did that happen?"

Eric looked at me with a loving smile and responded. "It is part of the Almighty's plan that every human being in His redeemed family has a guardian angel. I have been privileged to be yours, as well as to share God's love and concern with you."

I was speechless. I was loved. God was concerned about me. Eric was my guardian angel. He certainly was a true friend. Things here in Paradise Above kept getting better and better all the time!

"Eric," I whispered. I needed to find out more and was about to ask him more questions when another voluminous sound arose from the assembled Rubs alerting me to the happenings on that massive black stage.

Just behind the stage above it descended a silver like screen unfolding down from the ceiling of the Assembly Hall. It reached to the floor behind the stage and stopped. "What was this for," I wondered. "Eric, I'm sorry to be asking you so many questions. You have been really patient with me. I am really grateful for your help," I said thankfully, "but just what is that screen, is it part of the program?"

"I'm sure you will like it One Fifty-Five," Eric replied with a whimsical smile which brightened his handsome broad face.

"Well, Eric, what is it then?" I asked somewhat impatiently, as I thought perhaps he might be dealing with me in a playful manner.

"You will see in time," he said.

I could see some twinkles in his eyes, and I knew then that this was intended to be a playful conversation. "Tell me now Eric,"

I begged. "I certainly have no idea for what that screen can possibly be used."

"You certainly will be surprised," he firmly stated.

"Well, Eric." I could not get off my spoken retort, for as I began to continue with this pleasant conversation, a hushed silence fell across the great hall. Suddenly, unexpectedly silence now reigned.

Beyond the elevated stage and to its side, a door opened from the wall. I cannot remember seeing a door there. I thought that I had pretty well surveyed the assembly hall since our arrival, and could not recall seeing a door at that particular spot. "Oh well," I thought, "what does it matter anyway? It seemed like every eye was fixed upon that open door. Not a word was spoken by anyone, anywhere in that massed assembly. I wasn't sure what suspense was, but it seemed to me, that at this very time, I was experiencing it first hand. Any thoughts I had concerning the unfolded screen had rapidly disappeared from my mind.

Without warning, Eric who was sitting next to me, quickly rose to his feet and stood still. He stood tall and straight. I heard a noisy shuffling of feet and noticed that every Eric in the whole place had risen in unison with Eric. They were facing the open door located by the side of the stage. Expressions of great expectancy shone on every face!

Before I knew what was occurring, a sounding gasp echoed across the hall, as if to announce the entrance of some unusual event or distinguished guest. A figure came through the door. It was another Eric. But wait, he was dressed like an Eric with the white robe, but instead of a golden sash about his waist, he wore a golden girdle on his breast. He was taller than any of the Erics, including my own. Golden-colored hair adorned his head and his face was very much similar to all the other Erics. Yet, there was something about his appearance that was distinctive. He strode along the stage to the raised podium. As he walked, I noticed a light about him, especially around his face and head. That is what was different about him, I decided, for the other Eric's did not have his golden characteristic glow.

Eric and all the other Erics were still standing. I pulled a bit on Eric's robe to get his attention. As he looked down at me, I ventured a question. "Eric."

"Not now," Eric whispered as he quickly silenced me with a stern look upon his face.

"Welcome all of you Rubs. Welcome to all of you Erics," came a resounding voice from that special Eric who was speaking as he came to the podium. "We are so happy to have you here for your first session at the Celestial Academy. Please be seated with your Rubs," he requested.

While all the Eric's were being seated, the Eric at the podium continued to speak, "You have already noticed, I'm sure, that I am an Eric also. I am an angel spirit being like all the Erics but my name is Gabriel.

An outburst of conversation ensued immediately as Rubs by the scores turned to question their respective Eric's.

This was my opportunity to pursue the question I was about to ask Eric earlier. "Eric," I asked hurriedly. "Who is Gabriel? If he is an Eric, why is his name different from yours?"

"Gabriel," responded Eric, "means man of God, or one who stands in the presence of God-The Almighty One."

I wanted to ask more questions, but Eric kept talking and I knew that I should not interrupt him.

"Gabriel is one of God's choice messengers, and has been involved in so many special missions and tasks. He always glows with that golden light as you see around him now. He is often in the presence of the Lord who is a great Light. He is special also to all the Erics. We greatly love and respect him as God's special envoy," he concluded rapidly.

Gabriel had paused in his speaking to allow for the conversations pursuing the announcement of his name. He began to address the assembly again. "As all of you know, for your Eric's have shared this with you, this session is the first of many. Each session will prepare you better to live in Paradise Above, and help you to understand, most of all, who the Almighty One is and what He has done and is still doing today."

Gabriel paused for a moment again to provide some time for the Rubs to consider what he had just said. These sessions are really going to be interesting, I thought. Not only will I have many of my questions answered, but I will even learn more about Paradise Above and the Almighty One. Hopefully, more than I had ever expected.

"You will be learning about the Almighty One's history, both on the Earth below and in the Heavenlies Above," Gabriel announced with an assuring gesture, as he waved his hand out over the attentive audience. "Remember now," he continued, "to be able to recall your Rub number and do not forget it, although that is impossible here, for once you learn something you will always be able to remember it. Yes," he continued as he lowered his hand to the podium, "you will remember everything that you will hear and see during these sessions. You will, in most cases, understand also both what you hear and see presented in these sessions."

He then stepped away from the podium and walked towards the front of the stage area. Every eye followed his every movement. He was an impressive angel spirit.

I wondered how old he was, and if he had been in the presence of the Almighty One for all of that time. What stories he could relate to us. Gabriel stopped just on the edge of the stage and stooped down a bit to be more at the eye level view of his audience. He drew a deep breath, faced the audience, and turned his head slowly from one side of the hall to the other side, looking directly into the faces of the Rubs and Erics assembled in the great Celestial Academy Hall. He had our attention. Silence was obvious, not a word was heard anywhere throughout the assembly. We were waiting to hear his next pronouncement, but Gabriel said nothing. Instead, his hand came forth extended, and he began to point to all the areas in the assembly. Every one followed his every movement. Not a sound broke the silence. Finally, he looked up, stopped his pointing, and said, "Perhaps you will recall that earlier as you entered the hall to be seated, you noticed a fragrant aroma that grew more detectable as you sat down. Then, as you viewed the Hall, you noticed a glowing, golden light that filtered the air about you and invaded your very presences," he reminded us.

I remembered all of that just as he had said. At the time I noticed it, the light and scent, I wondered what it was, but quickly dismissed it when the stage, podium, and screen came into view.

"I want you to know," said Gabriel, "that someone special is here to assist you and guide you in your sessions and at other times regarding your learning process here in Paradise Above. Although you cannot see Him, you know He is here by your own awareness of His very presence. He is the Holy Ghost, the Spirit of God who proceeds from The Almighty One. He will be your final, infallible Teacher and Friend. He will instruct and guide you through your inner self," concluded Gabriel, as he turned and proceeded to assume his position at the podium.

I looked at Eric. He returned my look with his familiar smile and stated, "Yes, 155, the Holy Spirit is everywhere, and you will learn to love and cherish Him even as you will the Father and the Son."

I had much to learn let alone to assimilate-the Almighty One, the Father, the Son, and the Holy Spirit. I knew somehow that they were very important to me and everyone else in this hall. I knew that I was here to learn about them just as Gabriel had said.

I looked at Eric again and said, "I think I'm beginning to understand a few things."

Eric said nothing, nodded his head, acknowledged my statement, and looked again to the podium.

Gabriel, while still at the podium, gave his concluding statement, "Now we can proceed with our first session in your learning process."

"What can that be?" I wondered as a mounting feeling of anticipation raced through my mind.

CHAPTER 7

The Beginning

Conversations spread across the Great Academy Hall. It appeared that every Rub was in close dialogue with his Eric. What would we do and where would we be without our Erics? The questions flashed across my mind. How helpful Eric had been to me. I knew, of course, that all of the Rubs must feel as I do regarding their individual personal angel.

Gabriel had left the stage. There was much conversation in the hall, as the Rubs had so many questions to be answered. So without hesitation we all began to look to our Erics for answers.

"Eric do you know what is coming next?" I asked somewhat hurriedly, while expecting an explanatory response from him.

"I surely do not know," Eric responded. "Don't you recall this is my first time here also?" looking to me with that look of 'don't you remember me telling you that' all over his face.

"Yes, Eric, I'm sorry-you did tell me that," I sheepishly replied, tucking my chin to my chest to avoid seeing the look in his eyes. I knew he was looking at me.

"That's all right One Fifty-Five, I understand. Remember you are supposed to recall everything. Depend upon that!"

"But, Eric, haven't you been at least briefed about these meetings and the process?" I asked, somewhat puzzled as whether he knew what was going on at all.

"Yes, I've been briefed, but only on the overall process. I know very little about the details of the sessions," he shared with me.

Eric continued speaking, but his voice turned to a whisper as he looked from me to the stage area. "One Fifty-Five, it's about the Bible." His voice trailed off. I looked to the stage. The hall had become very quiet. Two figures entered from the door beside the stage area and strode swiftly across the stage to the podium.

Immediately I recognized Gabriel, but the other person I had never seen. He was a very imposing person. I knew from looking at him that he was not an Eric, nor even an angel like Gabriel. He wore the white robe with a golden sash, but his appearance was not the same. His hair was black and hung just above his massive shoulders. He face was broad with high cheekbones, a straight nose and a chiseled chin. His complexion was ruddy, as if he had been exposed to the outdoors for long periods of time. He was tall. He appeared to be a man of great force. Yes, he certainly looked impressive, but what I noticed most about him were his eyes. They were young eyes, but they had the deep gaze of ancient wisdom.

"Eric."

"Not now," he whispered. "Pay attention to what is happening, will you?" Eric asked me while avoiding my look and desire to talk.

"All right," I responded, as I redirected my attention to the stage area where Gabriel and this imposing man stood.

Gabriel was speaking, "I have the distinct pleasure and privilege to introduce to you the man that the Almighty One, God Himself, raised up to receive His Law, but most importantly inspired him to write the first five Books of the Holy Bible, God's Word, the Scriptures. I present to you, Moses."

A great, thunderous applause erupted from within the huge chamber. Every Eric in the hall stood to his feet as they applauded Moses the great Law-giver. Somehow, I knew that I should stand and join this expression of honor for Moses. Evidently all the other Rubs sensed that this was the appropriate action to take also, for as

I peered around the building, I could see everyone was standing and applauding. It was an exhilarating time. Obviously, this Moses is a very special individual indeed.

Moses raised his hand to motion the stopping of applause, and waved it slowly downward to indicate that it was time to sit down. Gabriel had already left the stage area and was nowhere to be seen. The audience was reclined and quiet, waiting for Moses to speak.

We waited. Moses said nothing, but slowly looked around the hall as if seeking to look into the eyes of every Rub present. Presently he stopped, put his hand into a compartment that was in the podium, and drew out a black box-like object which he held in his right hand, waving it high over his head.

"This Book you see held in my hand is the Bible that Gabriel spoke about earlier," Moses said as he paused to allow for that information to be absorbed. "This is the Book that tells us about God, the Almighty One. It tells about His dealings with people and spirit beings in the earth below as well as in the heavenlies above," he declared authoritatively.

It was obvious to me that Moses was sincere in his proclamation about the Bible, and it began to dawn on me that this was probably why we Rubs were here, that is, to learn about the Bible.

"Keep thinking, One Fifty-Five," Eric said quietly. "You are definitely on the right track," he said as he nudged my arm with that familiar personal touch of his.

"Rubs," Moses hesitated before continuing." You are very special. We welcome you to Paradise Above, and know that it will not be too long before you understand all that has happened and will be happening to you in the time ahead."

He paused again. He lifted the black Bible over his head again, and said, "This Book will be your way of better understanding all that you are experiencing." His voice trailed off, even as all the Rubs must be thinking as I thought- "how can that Bible help me?"

Moses must have read my mind.

"You know, in Paradise Above, we all speak and understand the same language. Well, this Book is written in that language, and you will soon discover that you are able to read it. This Bible will inform you all that one needs to know. You will find it exciting reading which will draw you closer to the Almighty One, your fellow Rubs, and personal Eric," he concluded, as he laid the Bible on top of the podium. "By the way," he said, as if he had already forgotten to tell us something, "you will receive a red-covered Bible of your own upon leaving the hall. You will be expected to read the first five books before our next session." He paused again, and then added, "Your Eric will explain all of this to you, and will always be available for assistance."

A red Bible of my own that I will be able to read! Already I felt a great desire to read it, and I did not yet posses the Book. I was excited just thinking about learning about God and in learning more about all of us.

"Eric," I started to say, but hesitated because Moses was still standing by the podium and it appeared that he was going to say more. Instead he walked over to a nearby chair and sat down. I wondered if he needed a break even as we did, but more than likely he sat down so that we might have some time to communicate with our Eric.

Again as before, all the Rubs began talking to their Erics. The assembly hall was an active chamber of vocal communications. Yet, for all the talking in such close quarters, strangely the noise level was quietly subdued. It was as if Eric and I were the only ones talking. Turning to Eric and catching his attention by pulling on his robe, I asked him what I was eager to know earlier but hesitated, "Eric."

"Yes, One Fifty-Five."

"Eric, please understand what I'm going to ask you is mostly a curious question on my part. Don't answer me if you desire not to do so," I insisted.

"Well, ask on."

"Are you sure?" I said timidly seeking his assurance.

"Go on and ask what more do you need?"

"Well, Eric, have you ever read the Bible through to completion?" I uttered hurriedly, not knowing what kind of answer I would get, or even if I would receive one.

"Why, of course I have read it," Eric quickly answered. He did look surprised that I had asked him such a question. I believe that he thought that I should have taken that for granted, as an expression of disappointment briefly appeared on his countenance. It vanished almost as fast as it had appeared. "Every angel was required to read the Bible, even as you are required to read it," Eric stated in a rather matter of fact voice. "But," he continued, "the Bible is such an amazing reading that I've read it numerous times-more than I can count. The Bible tells me about God, the Almighty One. It tells me about all that He has done, is doing, and will do in the future. Essentially the Bible tells the reader all God wants one to know."

"But Eric, don't all the Erics know about God just naturally? After all don't you have access to Him while you are here in Paradise Above?" I queried, feeling a bit proud of myself for asking such a profound question.

Eric did not answer me, but instead directed my attention back to the podium where Moses was again standing. All conversations ceased as those in the hall turned their respectful attention to him.

The lights in the great chamber began to dim. Then Moses addressed us saying, "We are now going to embark upon a Biblical adventure, starting at the beginning of the universe. You will be reading about this in detail in your red Bible, but while you are in these sessions you will be presented with general information in audible and visual form on the celestial screen. You will see what took place as if you were there yourself-this is quite a privilege-certainly your Eric will inform you in the time ahead as to why this is so." Moses raised his hand again above his head, and waved it as if to say goodbye. The lights were now off. Moses had been engulfed in the darkness, and all that remained to be seen was this gigantic screen before us.

A voice pierced the silence and the screen came alive with lights, and forms. The voice sounded like that of Moses, but I could not be sure.

"In the beginning God created the heavens and the earth and all that is therein. In six days He did this, creating everything out of nothing. On the seventh day God rested," the voice stated emphatically.

As he was talking, I could see on the screen stars, planets, lights, the sun and moon appear out of space out of nothing. They instantly came into being. Then the Earth came into view with abundant vegetation. It was all so wonderfully beautiful. Then a man, called Adam, was created out of the dirt. All kinds of living creatures were alive and moving. Adam named them all. God then put Adam to sleep, and out of Adam's side God made a beautiful woman called Eve. He told them to marry and have other beings like them.

I was astounded at what I was witnessing. Everything was moving swiftly. I had little time to reflect upon what I was seeing and hearing. Talking to Eric was out of the question. I was completely absorbed in what was taking place on the screen. I felt as if I was right there with all of them, experiencing this myself. The monologue presented by the voice continued to speak. He told us that God had planted trees in the Garden of Eden or Paradise and that two of them were special. One was the Tree of Life and the other was the Tree of the Knowledge of Good and Evil. God told them not to eat of the Tree of Good and Evil for if they did they would surely die.

As he was talking, I could see it all happening on the screen. The garden, the trees, Adam and Eve were all there. Then in the scene there appeared a beautiful form-a serpent that beguiled Eve, and she and Adam ate the forbidden fruit. I could see that they were in great despair and recognized that they had sinned. They also looked at one another and knew they were naked. So, they put together leaves to wear to cover their bodies. All the while as I viewed this, the voice continued to relate the story of all these events.

Because of their sin, God cursed the Earth and all living creatures. He clothed Adam and Eve in coats of fur, and expelled them from the garden. Yet, He promised them that one day a redeemer would come to redeem them from the curse and their sin. But for now, sin was in the Earth and it affected all beings bringing forth death.

I was deeply moved by what I had just experienced. What magnificence was revealed, yet, what tragic events took place. This is why, I thought, we Rubs are to come to these sessions and study the red-covered Bible-so that we might know about God and His creation. I was ready for more. What a beginning of a story! I had to know more, even to the very end, that is, if there is an end.

The lights came on as suddenly as they went off. The screen was not there, but Moses was standing at the podium surveying all the Rubs. Most of us, if not all of the Rubs, were in a state of astounded silence. What we all had seen and heard was far more than what we had ever expected. For all of us it was a monumental time of personal edification.

"As you leave the assembly hall, please do it quietly," Moses announced. "You will want to begin to read, and study the first five Books of the Bible (Genesis, Exodus, Leviticus, Numbers, and Deuteronomy) before our next session. Your Eric will help you in your studies, and he will also inform you when the next session will be. But for now, this officially closes the first session of the Post-Earth School. We will see you soon," he concluded, as he raised his right hand above his head, and waved to us as we passed rank and file out of the assembly hall. Erics and Rubs together, we descended onto the broad trail outside to return to our special place. I couldn't help but think, "what is next?"

CHAPTER 8

The Red-Covered Bible

The stroll back to our special places seemed to go quickly. The Crystal River, flowing almost motionless, was now to our left as we exited the assembly hall. Looking to the front and rear of the caravan traveling along the broad trail, I could see each Rub carrying his red-covered Bible. It was quite a sight; row upon row of red robed Rubs accompanied by their white robed Eric.

I wondered, where were the Eric Bibles? Certainly they each must have one. Are they red-covered as ours? And if they don't carry them with them, where are they kept?

"Now, One Fifty-Five, you know the answer to some of those questions that you are thinking," Eric said, as he interrupted my thoughts. "Remember I told you that I've read the Bible numerous times. The same is true of all the Erics." He paused for a moment and then added, "by the way, our Bible is white-covered, and we keep and study them in our special place."

We were making good time and before I knew it, we had left the broad-trail road paralleling the river, and were traveling on the narrower trail that eventually would lead to my special place. There were fewer Rubs going with us, as by now most of them had departed on their own trails leading to their special places. Nevertheless, during the time I spent walking and thinking, I continued to be awed by the beauty surrounding me. One undoubtedly would always be aware of the uniqueness of Paradise Above-of its extraordinary aurora, and of its brilliance. It could never grow old nor be taken for granted. The longer you resided here, the more Paradise Above became an integral part of your very being. After all, it is one of the Almighty One's creative wonders. With that appreciative thought in my mind, I wondered how Adam and Eve felt after they had lost their Paradise.

"That's something you might be able to ask them someday," Eric quipped. "I could not tell you how they felt, but you know what cursed things happened to them, and all living creatures, when they were expelled from the Garden of Eden. You heard Moses tell you this even as it was portrayed on the Celestial Screen for all to see. When you study the first five Books of your Bible, I am sure you will realize more fully what a special place they lost. But their greater loss came when they forfeited their close fellowship with the Almighty One," Eric explained sadly.

"I can't wait to arrive at my special place," I stated enthusiastically.

"Why is that?" Eric asked.

"You know Eric, you can know my thoughts, can't you? You're just being nice to me. Isn't that so?" I responded knowingly.

Eric looked at me as if he was attempting to figure out how he would respond to what I had just said. His face became very serious. It was one of the few times I had seen that expression on his usually smiling, happy, and contented face.

"Evidently, One Fifty-Five," he paused as if to gather together the words to best speak to me, "I have unintentionally mislead you about this. I must say it is unfortunate that you believe this. It is partly my fault though." He hesitated again, looked me in the eye and continued, "Only God the Almighty One knows the thoughts of everyone. We Erics do not have that ability, nor does any other living being, be it humans or angels."

"But, Eric," I interrupted, "you know my thoughts. You have proven that before, haven't you?"

"Well, yes and no. You see, sometimes we Erics have special senses and limited abilities in that area, which God allows us to exercise at times as we relate to our Rubs. But be advised it is not all the time, in fact, in many instances you will have to initiate the process by thinking about me or desiring answers from me, information, and help while in Paradise Above. When that happens, then I can know your thoughts, although not completely. Other times I can exercise some angelic perceptions that give me insights into your thinking and circumstances so that I might be of the most assistance to you."

We soon stopped by the trail leading into my special place. "Thank you Eric for helping me to understand. It makes sense to me now," I replied in a subdued voice.

In a way it was a relief to know that not all of my thoughts were known to Eric. Yet, I found it remarkable that God knew everyone's thoughts. That fact, in and of itself, was incomprehensible to me. What a God, this Almighty One is, and to think that I'm here in His Paradise Above. I know one thing for sure-I am privileged. I am blessed, although I still had so many things to discover.

"One Fifty-Five, I am going to leave you now. You will know your way. It's not far," he said, as he pointed in the direction I should take. "You will know your place when you arrive," he assured me.

"Take some time to relax, to enjoy the essence of your place, and to sense the Spirit's presence in your midst." He stopped speaking and pointed to the Red-Covered Bible I held in my hand. "Don't forget to read It. Remember how you told me you are eagerly looking forward to reading It," he reminded me. "I'm going now. Think of me if you need me," he shouted as he left the ground and ascended above the trees out of my sight.

Eric was gone. I traveled along the trail, and just as Eric had said, when I reached a juncture in the trail, I recognized it as the one leading to my special place. I turned in and arrived almost immediately at the most beautiful spot that I now call my place.

It was good to be home. Here in the garden place, I felt very much at ease even though I was alone. But then, I thought, not really alone, for the Almighty One knows my thoughts and his abiding Spirit is everywhere. The assurance of this was extremely comforting.

I located the lounge area by the nearby tree, and sat down, and began reading my Red- Covered Bible. Do those on Earth below have Bibles to read? I wondered about this. After awhile, I came to the conclusion that they did have a Bible. After all, that is why I'm learning about It now, for evidently I did not have an opportunity to read It before I came to Paradise Above. Evidently, they do.

As I opened the Bible for the first time, there came over me a great sense of reverence. The fact that it is a very special Book permeated my mind indelibly as I began briefly to thumb through its Pages. All the Rubs were told that this book was the Word of God, the Almighty One. God took great pleasure in those who read His Book. I want Him to be pleased with me, I thought as I prepared to read.

The first Book in that Book of Books was Genesis followed by Exodus, Leviticus, Numbers, Deuteronomy and thirty-three more Books until Malachi, which completed the Old Testament. The next set of Books was the New Testament, starting with Matthew and ending with Revelation.

There were certainly many Books to be read. I was thankful, as of now, upon seeing all those Books that I had just been assigned the first five Books to read. As I turned to Genesis and read 'in the beginning God created the heaven and the earth,' all that I had heard and seen at my first session in the Celestial Assembly Hall came back into my memory like a rushing flood of waters. Vividly, in my minds eye, I could see the screen and view all that was portrayed upon it.

I was reading quickly and comprehended most of all that I read. Evidently this Book was written in the heavenly language, and we Rubs were especially adept in it. So, my reading continued to be extra fast, very informative, and completely exhilarating. This was God's Book.

Already I was in love with my Red-Covered Bible. I desired to be a student of His Words. I realized there was so much to know and to understand. Just that thought alone was overwhelming.

The reading was fascinating, God pronouncing the curse; Adam and Eve driven from the Garden of Eden; Eve's sons; Abel and Cain, bringing sacrifices to God; Abel's blood sacrifice being accepted by God while Cain's sacrifice of the fruits of the ground was rejected; Cain killing his brother (probably because of jealousy) and consequently banned from the family, Cain becomes a vagabond on the face of the Earth bearing the mark of Cain; meanwhile the Earth is populated with persons who live for many years, even hundreds of years; the Earth becomes a place of turmoil as the sons of God see the daughters of men and take them as wives; giants also dwelt upon the earth and God saw that all of them had committed wickedness and entertained evil imaginations in their minds. Then the Bible said the Lord changed His mind about this creation of His when "the Lord said, I will destroy man whom I have created from the face of the earth; both man, and beast, and the creeping thing, and the fowls of the air; for it repenteth me that I have made them."

I was puzzled, had not I seen on the Celestial Screen all that God had created, and had not I even heard His pronouncement regarding it, that "it was very good"? Now God was about to destroy what He had created? How can that be? I thought. I really did not understand. I closed my Red-Covered Bible, and set it down on the table next to my lounge chair. I got up and began walking around my place pondering over what I had just read.

A mental picture of Eric invaded my mind. I have missed him, but now that I could use his assistance he is not here. Thinking about him and my puzzlement over my Bible reading should bring him to my side. I was sure of it and so I thought to talk to him quietly in my mind. No sooner had this thought transpired then Eric stood there right beside me!

"Sorry One Fifty-Five," Eric said, nudging my shoulder with his bent arm, as he so customarily did, "but it took me a little longer than I expected to arrive here with you."

"Well, I'm glad you're here," I said, with no desire on my part to know why it took him longer than usual to respond to my need or call.

"Eric, you know about my puzzlement over some things I have read," I stated hesitantly, "don't you?" I questioned.

"Look," Eric replied. "You stopped reading at a critical point in the Bible. You should have continued to read beyond that point, and you would have immediately seen the plan of God for His creation," he explicitly stated, as he walked to my lounge table, picked up my Bible and turned to the passage I had just completed.

Eric, with the open Bible, turned toward me and with an insistent tone in his voice and said, "Sit down and read the rest of the passage from here," as he pointed to the verses with his extended finger.

I did as he said, took the Bible, and sat down to continue my reading. It was there. God's plan was to start anew with Noah, his family, and with representative creatures of every kind. These creatures were sheltered in the massive ark throughout the great, disastrous flood. Every animal and person died except those that were in the ark. God declared then that He would never again bring a "flood to destroy the earth" and said "I do set my bow in the cloud, and it shall be for a token of a covenant between me and the earth."

"Tell me, One Fifty-Five," Eric abruptly startled me with an opening question, for I had momentarily forgotten his presence. I was so absorbed in my reading of the Bible that his speaking voice jolted me. Eric continued with his question, "do you have some clarity in your thoughts in understanding the events you have just read?"

"Yes, Eric, very much so."

"But I still detect some puzzlement on your part, is that not so?"

I looked at Eric, and his eyes focused on mine. I could see that he desired to help me. Now hopefully, I could express myself adequately to him. "Eric, I can see from reading that wickedness and evil thoughts by men caused God to bring such judgment upon his own creation, is that correct?" I ventured.

"Yes, exactly One Fifty-Five," Eric responded in a complimentary tone. "You see wickedness and evil imaginations are all sin in God's sight. God abhors sin. He is sinless, Holy and pure. Sinful persons and sinful things caused God to exercise His judgment and consequently His wrath. But this time He has decided to deal with men and His creation differently than before the flood. You will see this in so many obvious ways as you continue to read from your Bible, and as you regularly attend your sessions in the Celestial Assembly Hall," concluded Eric, while catching his breath and ending his statement with a long-winded sigh.

"Have I sinned and done evil, Eric?" I asked impulsively, for I had never given it any thought until now. For some reason the question just darted out of my mouth.

"No, not at all," Eric quickly replied with a reassuring voice. He paused as if he was contemplating something of a deep nature.

I felt he was trying to decide whether he was going to reveal something to me or not. Eric's face became quite somber. Nevertheless, he remained quiet. I suppose he was indulged in thoughtful meditation. Still, he did not speak. Rather he got up from his chair, and proceeded to walk toward the sparkling pond near the other edge of the garden.

"Eric," I shouted, "is there something wrong?"

Eric turned toward me, took a few steps, and summoned me to come to him. I got up from the lounge and walked over to where he was standing.

"Come, let's take a stroll," he softly commanded as he put his hand on my shoulder. "I have a few things to tell you."

I didn't say a word. We began walking around my beautiful space. All the while I was waiting for him to talk to me about these things. Slowly Eric began to speak again.

"No, One Fifty-Five, you did not commit sin, nor have you done evil, you can be sure of that," he stated emphatically. "But others involved with you on Earth below did commit sin and cause evil things to occur," he paused, and then said, "many people below were affected by it-even you." We stopped now under one of the towering trees. He faced me and continued to talk.

"Remember a while back how we talked about you being killed, unborn and dead?"

"Yes, I do," I responded, "and that is why I'm called a Rub-Redeemed Unborn Baby, right?"

"That's for sure. You did not forget," he congratulated me. "But then how could you ever forget," Eric retorted. "Remember how we talked of God's love for you," he asked me, "and how He gave you a tabernacled body, and placed you here in Paradise Above?"

"Yes," I replied, "and I am constantly grateful to Him for that."

"Well, God did that for you in spite of the sins of others there on earth. But you see they broke God's moral law, and took it upon themselves to kill you-to cause your death before you were ever allowed to be birthed into that world below as a vital living human being." Eric halted, took a deep breath and continued, "One Fifty-Five they denied you your right to life. That is their great sin, not yours-and consequently you are a Rub."

I thought long upon what Eric said. There was only silence now between us. I could hear the water bubbling in the pond. The leaves in the trees were trembling as a wisp of breeze caressed them. "I was killed, dead, unborn, but how? Eric, how was I killed?"

"I don't think that I am at liberty to discuss that with you just now. Please do not ask me more about it. I promise you in due time and at the right time you will know."

I looked at him inquiringly.

"Trust me, One Fifty-Five," he stated.

I knew instinctively that I could trust Eric and to take him at his word. "All right Eric, but will it be soon?" I questioned.

"It should be One Fifty-Five."

It was quiet again. Only the sounds emanating from my special place could be heard. Eric and I both seemed to have dropped off into our own private thoughts.

"Look," the silence was interrupted, "I've got to be going now," Eric announced. "Pick up some more on your reading and discover more of God's dealings with Noah, his family and the peoples of the earth after the Flood. You will not only find it factual but, completely fascinating." Eric completed his dialogue with me as he again raised his arms and began to ascend up beyond the trees. As he departed into the blue the thought that I now had embedded in my mind so vividly was-how was I killed?

CHAPTER 9

Robert and Jeni

The thought kept bouncing back into my mind, 'How was I killed? Was it a sin?' I have no recollection of my "so-called," death so I was unable to rely upon any memories of it that I may have had. Eric reassured me that I would be told more sometime in the near future. At least that was somewhat comforting. With this in mind, I determined to dismiss those questions from my mind as quickly as they arose. After all, I could not answer them, so why should I attempt to deal with them? I thought to myself, "better now that I should do other things." Going back to the lounge area where I could continue with my readings seemed the best thing to do. So on the way there, I picked a couple of brightly-colored orange fruits to eat during my reading. I sat down, picked up my red covered Bible, took a few bites from one of the fruits, and turned to Noah's people re-populating the Earth to commence my reading.

It was very interesting to me to read that they all had the same language, just as we have here in Paradise above. But God confused their tongues and scattered them abroad over all the face of the Earth, for along with Nimrod and the masses, they displeased God by their behavior, and desired to build a tower of Babel to Heaven. During this dispersion, I could see that God had a special plan for Earth and its people, as He began to deal with Abram and his family.

I closed the Bible and thought for awhile. Did this plan that I could see taking place, have any affect upon all of us that are now here in Paradise above? Of course, I could not answer my own question, but I felt there had to be some connection, some correlation, especially when God made that covenant with Abraham about his seed, about a mighty nation out of his loins and that all people would surely be blessed because of God's promise. It was exciting to read of God's dealings with Abraham and his descendants-to see the circumstances of their lives and how through their faith in God they triumphed in and over them. I took some more bites from the delicious fruits which I had picked and again resumed my readings.

The story of the mistreatment of Joseph by his jealous brothers and their devious plan to deceive Jacob as they sold Joseph into slavery was especially annoying to me. I thought, "how can God bless that situation?" But as I continued to the conclusion of that story, it was Joseph's statement that answered that question for me when he addressed his penitent brothers and said, "ye meant it for evil, but God meant it for good." I laid the Bible down and the thought occurred to me that God knew what He was doing in His relationships with His world and His creation. I looked at how far I had progressed in my readings as I ran my thumb along the edge of the pages. It was not very far. I had much more to read, but at least I had finished reading Genesis one of the first five Books of the Bible I was assigned to read. I stood up and began walking around my space just to see if there was anything, I needed to do to keep it dressed. Everything appeared in its pristine state. Nothing seemed out of place. Nevertheless, I transversed the entire garden, which was considerable in size, while observing all that was around me. As I approached a group of fruit trees adjacent to the trail that led out of my place, I noticed among those trees bordering my space the movement of a Red-Robed person. It must be another Rub. It certainly was not an Eric. I slipped through a small opening under the trees and through the flowering bushes into another garden space which was identical to mine. It was complete with fruit trees, towering green trees, and flowers with streams of flowing pond waters. It even had a lounge area like mine. I looked closely and noticed a Red-Covered Bible on one of the tables.

"Hello, there," a voice came from behind me. I looked around and saw the Red-Robed Rub that I had noticed just a few moments ago. "Well, hello," I replied. "I see that you are a neighbor of mine." "Yes, it appears that way," he said, as he approached me with a smile on his face and an outstretched hand. "It's good to meet you," I said as I shook his hand. "The same is true for me also," he replied, "it's really good to know that I have another Rub for a neighbor, that is, if you are a Rub, for you certainly look like one," he concluded with a curious look upon his countenance. "You definitely look like a Rub also," I said as I looked him over.

He was the same height as myself-perhaps a bit larger in the shoulders than I, but nevertheless we were about the same size. His face was light skinned, rather narrow with smiling hazel colored eyes, thin lips, a prominent nose and possessing a crop of wavy black hair upon his head. All in all, he had the appearance, of a pleasant handsome male being. And, as I thought of it, all the Rubs I have seen were pretty much the same in appearances with the exceptions of various skin complexions, and different eye and hair colors. One common feature though, for all of us, was our red-robed attire. "Yes, I am a Rub just like you," I responded happily realizing that my neighbor would very well become a friend. I would like that very much indeed I thought.

"Do you have a name?" he asked as we stood facing each other. "A name?"

"Yes," he reiterated, "a name."

"No, I don't have a name. You mean a name like Eric?" I asked. "Well, yes, like Eric's name, but of course not Eric. All the angel beings arc all named Eric," he said, rather matter of factly

"I'm sorry, but I don't have a name, at least as far as I know. Eric never related that to me," I replied somewhat bewildered. "Do you have a name?" I continued. "All I have is a number that Eric calls me. If that is a name then I have one. It's 155". I murmured rather sheepishly.

"Why, yes, I have a name," he responded, "but I also have a number." He paused, and then added thoughtfully, "that's strange that you do not have a name."

"Nevertheless, One Fifty-Five, it is good to meet you. I'm Robert, and my number is 22,643,002," he stated in a mild-mannered voice. "Nice to know you Robert, but shall I call you Robert or just Zero Zero two?" I inquired. "My Eric just uses the last three numbers of my number to address me. Does your Eric do the same?"

"Now that you mentioned it," he said, "my Eric seldom, if ever, calls me by my name Robert.... it's always Zero Zero Two."

"So we're just numbers here in Paradise Above, Robert," I guess. "There must be some reason for it," Robert replied. "Yes," I agreed. "Perhaps we will find out why very soon." We both continued to stand facing one another as we talked. I was puzzled over why I only have a number for a name while he, Robert, has both a number and a name. Yet in this short time since our meeting, I felt that there was a bonding taking place between us, for some reason unknown to me. I felt it strongly. Perhaps it's because we are neighbors and that is the way things are supposed to be in Paradise Above. "Say One Fifty-Five, let's sit down and talk some more. Come sit with me in my lounge area," he graciously invited, "in fact have a seat while I pick a few fruits for our enjoyment." He volunteered cheerfully as he wandered off toward the fruit trees.

I sat down while he was selecting fruit from the far side of his space. I picked up his Red-Covered Bible from the table and thumbed through it. I noticed that he had a bookmark inserted at the end of Genesis. I wondered if all of the Rubs are reading at the same pace. Probably so, so that when the next session occurs we will all be up to date, prepared for the next step in our process. I was congratulating myself for such progress when suddenly I noticed some movement behind me. I was surprised when I heard a sound near me. "Pardon me, is this your space?" came a questioned voice that sounded embarrassed. I rose up out of my chair so that I could fully turn to see who was talking to me.

"I'm so sorry to bother you, but somehow I've seemed to have wandered out of my space," she said apologetically.

This was the first time I had ever been addressed by a female human being, a female Rub to be exact. It was, to be certain, a different experience than communicating with Robert, or say, Zero Zero Two.

"No, this is not my space and you haven't disturbed me," I assured her. "My space," I continued, "is over there to the left." I pointed in the direction opposite from where we were standing.

"Oh," she said. "But whose space is this?"

"This space belongs to Robert," I replied. "He's over there at the far end of this space selecting some fruit to eat."

I pointed to where Robert was. She turned and located him walking under a clump of brightly-colored fruit trees. She turned back toward me. I could see then that she was not as tall as Robert or me. Nor was she of a form as large as us. She was fair skinned and her complexion appeared to be smoother and softer than mine. Her brownish-black, long hair glittered in the bright light and lay gently on her shoulders. Her face was oval in shape, adorned with full lips. A small but straight nose, and most noticeable of all, were her velvet-green eyes peering out from black eyelashes and arching eyebrows. She was strikingly attractive. Then I realized that all of the Rubs that I had seen and observed, whether they were male or female, were all handsome and attractive. That is not to say that all Rubs looked alike, similar maybe, especially since we were all clothed in red robes. But one could see the difference in skin color, complexions, eye and hair colors which enhanced each Rub's facial features and gave each one a distinct and individual entity.

"Well, perhaps you can help me," she addressed me with her voice, but with her questioning green eyes.

"I certainly will try," I promised, "but what is it that I can do?"

"Help me to return to my space." She paused, and looked around, stopped and pointed to the trail that led out of Robert's space. "I came in here on that trail thinking that this was my space, but as you can see, I was wrong," she admitted.

I looked at the trail and realized that it leads to a small commonly-used trail that eventually led to the broad road, which went to the Celestial Academy Hall. "Evidently you've been on the trail that leads to the broad road and you just missed your connecting trail leading to your space," I offered with an air of deductive logic.

"That sounds probably right," she replied, "but I also went into a space that was empty thinking it to be mine. I sat down in the lounge area, but then I noticed the Red-Covered Bible on the table. I knew immediately that this was not my space," she concluded with a sigh, while brushing away some strands of hair that had fallen over her cheekbone.

"Why is that?" I questioned.

"Because I left my Bible on the lounge chair," she exclaimed.

"That was more than likely my space that you were in. You must be my neighbor on the other side of my space," I expounded quite confidently.

"Let's go find your space," I insisted, "but first let me introduce myself. I'm called One Fifty-Five for short, or for whatever reason, that is what my Eric calls me," I said, while wondering where her Eric was. "Tell me," I questioned, "why did you not call on your Eric for help?"

"I probably should have. I guess I was embarrassed or thought I could find my own way. But look, I've met you, One Fifty-Five. Oh, forgive me," she hesitated and smiled, "my name is Jeni, and my number is Zero Zero Three. It's nice to meet you," she surmised.

"Say, what's going on here, One Fifty-Five?" questioned Robert, as he approached us holding a handful of fruit.

I did not notice Robert walking toward us. In fact, I had forgotten about him completely since my encounter with Jeni.

"Robert," I called back to him, "we have a neighbor. Hurry, come meet her."

It did not take Robert long to arrive, even though he stopped at the lounge area near where we were standing to discard the fruit he was carrying.

"Robert, this is Jeni and her number is Zero Zero Three," I said.

"It's a pleasure to meet you Jeni," replied Robert. "It's interesting, Jeni," he added, "that my number is Zero Zero Two."

"That's curious, isn't it?" she responded, as she looked to Robert and then to me as if she expected some type of an explanation from us. "I don't have an answer," Robert volunteered.

"Neither do I, Jeni. For the moment it doesn't seem that important, does it?" I asked.

"Probably not now," she responded, "but to me it's important that I return to my space."

"It sure is. Let's go then," I said, as I started toward the nearby trail with her following.

"Robert, why don't you come with us if that's okay with Jeni?" I asked.

"That sounds like a good suggestion," Jeni said smilingly, as she beckoned Robert to catch up with us as we walked toward the trail leading out of his space. We all reached the trail together, and began to walk down to the central trail. While we traversed the trail, I told Robert about meeting Jeni, and how she ventured out of her space, got lost, and eventually ended up in his space.

"Why doesn't she call upon her Eric for help?"

"She said that she was embarrassed and felt she could find her space without him," I replied.

"That's true," she confirmed. "I'm sorry to put out the both of you."

"That's no problem," we both chimed in. "This way all three of us have become friends," Robert stated with a cheerful smile and a glint in his eye.

"Yes, if she would have called on her Eric, this may not have happened," I offered. "Perhaps this was supposed to happen," I mused aloud, although I was thinking more to myself aloud than talking to them.

We arrived at the central trail quickly. Then it dawned on me that Robert's trail connected with my trail just before we arrived here, and undoubtedly Jeni's trail was the one on the right of my trail that we had just passed. "Let's take that trail to the right," I suggested.

"Why not?" Robert said.

"It looks like my trail alright," Jeni said with a confident look.

So we took the trail, all three of us, and almost instantly arrived at a space. There did not appear to be anyone occupying it, as we observed the entire space.

"Oh, this is it!" Jeni happily exclaimed, a broad, beaming smile lighting her attractive face. "There's my Red-Covered Bible on the lounge, just where I left it," she announced.

Both Robert and I were happy that Jeni was back in her space.

"Thank you, One Fifty-Five and Robert, for helping me. I really appreciate it," she said enthusiastically. All of us were relieved now that Jeni was back in her special place. As I surveyed her space, I could see instantly that it was almost identical to my space, as well as Robert's. "Evidentially all the spaces for Rubs were the same," I concluded.

"That's right, One Fifty-Five, they are all the same, one beautiful space after another,"

My Eric spoke to me. As I looked up toward that familiar sounding voice above, I could see Eric descending down from the towering trees. But he was not alone. There were two more Erics descending with him. They all arrived together. My Eric was leading, accompanied by both Robert's and Jeni's Erics. All three of us were surprised at their coming but, we were still very happy to see them. The Erics greeted us and had a number of things to share with us separately. Then my Eric addressed all of us, for it appeared that, at least on this occasion, he was the major spokesman.

"We're glad that you have met one another. After all, you are neighbors. All the special personal spaces are triangular in shape, and they are adjacent one to another in groups of threes," he paused, caught his breath, looked at the other Erics for their approval and continued. "All the Rubs live in these threesome groupings," Eric paused again, cleared his throat, looked at me and said, "One Fifty-Five, your space is in the center. Robert's is on your left as you face the trail leading to the central trail, and Jeni's space is on your right. Robert's and Jeni's trail lead into your trail. So you will be able to visit one another as you desire, and even travel together for you sessions," he concluded. That information was good to know. In fact, perhaps I could gather more information while all three Erics were present. I wanted to find out why I didn't have a name, and why Robert's and Jeni's numbers were Zero Zero Two and Zero Zero Three. "Not now, One Fifty-Five, another time," Eric abruptly stated, as he read my thoughts. "The next session is coming very soon. You need to return to your own spaces, get your Bibles and be prepared to go when we arrive at your places," he said. He and the other two Erics ascended out of our midst into the blue above those towering trees and out of our sight.

CHAPTER 10

Another Session

We had all been gathered together, Robert, Jeni, and I with our individual Erics to attend the next session in our on going process. We were walking along the familiar trails leading to the Assembly Hall, and were accompanied by numerous other Red-Robed Rubs.

As we reached the broad trail road that paralleled the Crystal River and turned left, I began thinking how eagerly I was looking forward to this next session.

"Eric," I asked breaking the silence among our little group. "Do you know if the rest of the first five Books of the Bible will be presented?"

Eric looked at me without stopping and said, "Why do you ask that, One Fifty-Five?"

"I'm curious," I replied.

"Now that One Fifty-Five has mentioned it, I'm curious too," commented Robert.

"Me too!" exclaimed Jeni.

With that being said, I could see the Erics quietly communicating with one another over probably how to answer my question, if at all. There was more silence as we continued toward the Academy. It was now visible in the distance.

"Look you guys," Robert's Eric addressed us. "You know this will be our second session, just like yours. It's not like we have been going to many of these ourselves and know completely what is going on."

"Yes, that's true," added Jeni's Eric, "but our thought is that the session will cover from the end of Genesis to the end of Deuteronomy."

"After all, you've finished reading Genesis, along with the rest of the Rubs, and the other four Books in preparation for this session," added my Eric emphatically.

From that pronouncement, I believe that Robert, Jeni and I received the message that the question had been sufficiently answered. Again we lapsed into silence as we approached the magnificent and massive Celestial Academy. The doors opened quietly. We entered into the spacious lobby, proceeded through it, and took our seats in the main auditorium. Nothing had changed. The atmosphere of fragrance and the special lighting was still here. There was also that deep and knowing feeling that one had of the presence of the Almighty One. He was in our midst.

Robert, Jeni and I looked around the hall. To me the hall looked larger than when I was here before. There appeared to be more Rubs seated with their Eric as compared to our last session.

"Is this the same auditorium we were in during our last session? It looks the same but it appears to be larger," I asked Eric.

"It's the same place but they have opened up an adjoining wing to accommodate more people," responded Eric.

"Oh," I nodded.

"That's the same question I entertained," expressed Robert, who evidently overheard our conversation. After all, we were all seated next to one another so it was rather easy to overhear one's comments and conversation.

"I wonder why there are more people?" blurted out Jeni.

I looked to Jeni and noticed that her Eric was probably going to answer her question. But just then the lights dimmed. Jeni's Eric remained silent though, as well as the rest of the Rubs and Erics within the great hall. Then all of the Erics in the hall stood to attention applauded as Gabriel, followed by Moses, appeared on the stage. I stood also and joined the applauding. So did every red-robed person in the hall. The ovation was thunderous, and rightly so, for we all realized how great a man was this Moses, who was used mightily by God. After awhile, Gabriel came to the podium and asked us to take our seats.

The hall was quiet. I could sense among the attendees an air of eager anticipation.

"Welcome to our second session," announced Gabriel. "I know you all have kept your reading assignments. You are to be commended!" he continued. "You are again in for a rewarding time of learning from our teacher for today, Moses." Gabriel turned toward Moses and motioned for him to take the podium. As Moses approached the podium, the large screen descended from above and unfolded behind him. The lights were all but off, and all that was visible was Moses and the illuminated screen.

Moses stood tall and resolute as he spoke to us saying, "I too wish to welcome you back again for our second session," he paused briefly, turned to the screen behind him and said, "you will soon see all that can be read in your Red-Covered Bibles from Genesis through Deuteronomy and beyond. It will be vividly displayed and clearly voiced on this big screen.

He turned back to us, raised both of his arms above his head with his face and palms turned upward, and said in a resounding voice, "thank you God for allowing me the privilege of sharing with these the wonders of Who You are, of how You displayed Your wonders to the world and used me, an unworthy person, as an instrument to fulfill Your marvelous purposes in your dealings with men."

Not a noise, nor a voice, nor even the sound of breathing could be heard in the great hall for it was as if everyone had spontaneously held his breath. We all were seated breathlessly, captured by the awesomeness of it all. I was deeply moved by what he said. I recalled some of the writings in the Books of the Red-Covered Bible, and knew from them that Moses was a giant of a man for God. I thought, now what we were about to see and hear will be mostly about God and Moses.

Sure enough, I was right! Before my very own eyes I saw and heard everything, scene by scene, as it transpired so long ago. There were the twelve Tribes in Egypt with their leaders; the eventual slavery into which they were cast; the death of Joseph and the leader of Egypt. Then there was a new leader with his persecution of the infants born of Hebrew women. What a grim scene to behold! Next was Moses as a baby being set adrift in a basket, and rescued by Pharaoh's daughter from the Nile River. He was raised as her own son in the royal household. Moses was then depicted as a grown man departing from Egypt after he killed an Egyptian, because the man was beating one of his Hebrew brethren. Moses lived in a foreign place, became married, had children and while in the desert he had a burning-bush meeting with God. God commissioned Moses to return to Egypt. Along with his brother, Aaron; they petitioned the Egyptian king to free the children of Israel. The king refused to allow the Hebrew nation to leave his country. God allowed terrible catastrophes and plagues to trouble the Egyptian population, with the final plague killing the firstborn of each Egyptian family.

As I observed all that was occurring on the screen, I could not understand why Pharaoh battled the Lord. Did he not know that he could not win?

We saw everything in vivid and realistic presentations, but they passed so quickly that we had little time to absorb, yet alone mediate upon what we were viewing.

Finally, upon the death of his son, Pharaoh summoned Moses and told him to take the Hebrew nation and depart from the land.

Watching those Hebrews, millions of them, leave the land with gifts and their belongings was a treat to the eyes. God's delivery of His people was victorious as they fled from Egypt. However, they were still not safe. Pharaoh changed his mind, and with an army of men and chariots swiftly pursued the fleeing nation. They caught up with the Hebrews on the banks of the Red Sea. The helpless Hebrews were trapped. They followed Moses, their leader, willingly, but now they were surrounded by the troops of the Pharaoh. On one side of them was the sea, and on the other was Pharaoh's army!

Upon the screen we saw a pillar of great blazing, fire appear between Pharaoh's troops and the Hebrews, preventing Pharaoh's approach. Then I saw Moses with his staff raised, standing and overlooking the Red Sea proclaiming with great confidence, "Fear ye not, stand still and see the salvation of the Lord which He will show to you today: for the Egyptians whom ye have seen today, ye shall see them again no more forever."

What I viewed next forever will be imbedded upon my memory. With a thunderous roar, a mighty wind came from the east and divided the sea's waters so that dry land appeared, and the waters were stacked up as walls on either side. Then that mass of people, the Hebrews, went onto that dry land in the midst of the sea, and safely arrived on the other shore. The scene was spectacular, and awakened in me my memory of viewing the violent and chaotic flood of Noah's day. (I knew about this for I had previewed the writings about Noah in the Red- Covered Book.) To view these occurrences personally made even a greater impression, not only upon my mind, but also upon my heart.

The scene that took place next was not only thrilling but tragic. Pharaoh's army, following after the fleeing Hebrews, was encompassed by the collapsing walls of water of the Red Sea. They all drowned- every one of them. There were no survivors. The Hebrews were now safe to follow after their Lord, and their deliverer Moses.

Not a whisper was detected in the whole auditorium. The images on the screen began to fade while the lights in the hall proceeded to brighten slowly. Moses stood facing us. Everyone remained silent. It had been an exhilarating presentation. We had again viewed the past just as it had happened.

"We will have an intermission for a short time," Moses announced, "then back to our seats for the end of today's session."

Loud speaking became apparent among all of the assembly, as the hall went from total silence to a multitude of conversations. As we arose from our seats in order to just stand for awhile Moses again addressed us saying, "Erics why don't you take your Red-Robed persons in to the main parlor during the recess? They will be able to socialize better there." Then Moses added another word, "We will let you know when to return to your seats for the rest of the session." At that, we all filed out with our individual Erics to the main parlor. What the main parlor was I had no idea. Eric nudged me and said, "Follow me One Fifty-Five, I know where it is."

As we went, I could see that Robert and Jeni with their Erics, were following along closely behind us.

We all spilled out into the main lobby along with hundreds of other Erics and Red-Robed Rubs. Eric led us to a hall just off of the lobby, and as we waited our turn to enter, I noticed that a lot of Rubs had different sash-like girdles about their waists. Their sashes were not white like mine or the other Rubs. They were gold and white. Just to be sure that I saw those colors, I turned to Robert behind me, "Robert, do you see those Rubs waiting in line?" I asked him.

"Not really," he replied.

"Look closer," I insisted.

Robert looked again. This time more carefully. "Why yes, One Fifty-Five, now that you mention it, the sashes about their waists are not the same color as ours. They are gold and white. Now what do you think about that?" he asked.

"I don't know, and I'm sure Jeni doesn't know, so don't bother to ask her." I answered.

Now we were standing in front of the door that split down the middle. Robert and I abruptly stopped our conversation. I looked to my Eric and was about to question him when he looked at me smilingly and said, "It's just an elevator. You walk in when the doors open and when they close the elevator takes you up or down in the Celestial Academy as you direct it with your voice." Eric spoke loud enough for all those around us to hear. Evidently Eric understood the puzzlement that the rest of the surrounding Rubs had concerning the doors that split down the middle, so he made his explanation loud enough to us so that those Rubs around us would hear also.

The doors opened. We entered into a large room. When the room was filled, the doors closed and Eric said, "main parlor please." The whole room, with all of us standing in it, went down. It, in a way, was like when Eric took me on a flight up above the trees, but this was going down. "The elevator is taking us to the bottom floors of the hall where the parlor is located," Eric stated. "There we will have our recess. When the elevator stops and the doors open, just follow me to the lounge area so we may sit and talk for awhile," Eric instructed us.

No sooner had Eric finished talking when the elevator stopped. The doors opened and we followed our Eric into a mammoth room. I knew we were inside a building and probably at the bottom of it, but what I was seeing was unbelievably familiar to me. It was my special place. In fact, as I surveyed the parlor, it seemed that everyone's special place was there-but in a smaller version. The fruit trees, the flowers, the bushes, and even the sparkling watery streams with their ponds were like those in my special place. Even down here the light was as it was outside the Celestial Academy. It was Paradise Above, without the towering trees, right here below.

We followed my Eric to one of the lounge areas and sat down. The table in the center of our sitting area was holding a large bowl of fruit. Drinking glasses and a large pitcher of water were also on the table. It did not take long for all of us to take advantage of the water and the fruit treats. For a while, not much was said, as all of us were occupied with eating. But Robert turned to his Eric, and I could see by the look on his face that he was going to ask a question about the Rubs we had observed just before we entered the elevator. "Eric, One Fifty-Five and I saw these Rubs by the elevator who looked like us but their sash girdles were different than others. Why the difference?" Robert's Eric looked at the other two Erics with a subtle smile on his face. He did not say a word. Finally Jeni's Eric, while ignoring us three Rubs, spoke to the other Erics saying, "Don't you believe that it's time for our humans to know?"

Again they looked at each other, but no audible verbal communication occurred between them. I knew they were speaking in a way that we Rubs were incapable of knowing. Some time had passed, and we sat there waiting for some type of a reply regarding Robert's question. My Eric was the first to speak. It appeared again that he was the major spokesman for our little group.

"One Fifty-Five, Robert, and Jeni," my Eric addressed us, as he set his glass on the table, stood up and walked to a position near us so that we could easily see and hear him. "We Erics believe that you will be able to understand what we are about to tell you, and that you will be able to assimilate this information in a way that will please the Almighty One." The other two Erics looked at us and nodded their heads in apparent agreement.

My Eric cleared his voice, took a deep breath, and began to answer Robert's question. Needless to say, we were very attentive even though the parlor was filled with sounds of speaking.

We tuned out all other noise, for we eagerly desired to hear what Eric was going to say. "Those Rubs," he pointed to some that were near us with his finger, and then waved his raised hand and motioned with it from one side of the parlor to the other. "You see them," he explained, "they have tabernacled bodies as you have, and they are male and female human beings as you." Again he paused. Eric was not the swiftest talker, but I think he was choosing his words carefully so that he could present the information in such a clear way that we would surely comprehend what he was about to say. "All of these that you call Rubs have names, like yours, but for different reasons. Robert, you were named but you were never born. The same is true for you Jeni. And you, One Fifty-Five, were never given a name, so you just have a number," again he paused while speaking. "But all three of you do have numbers for various reasons which we will be able to explain later, not now." Eric stopped speaking. He stepped toward the table, picked up his glass of water and said, "Excuse me. I need a little water. My mouth seems to be getting dry." I wondered if he was nervous, but I thought Erics don't get nervous, but they are sensitive, especially in relationships that deal with their assigned human beings.

Eric drank, put the glass down, stepped back to his original place, and said, "These Red-Robed tabernacled beings have a different background and history than what you and other Rubs have here in Paradise Above."

Eric cleared his voice again, shuffled his feet, looked around the parlor, looked directly at each of us, and in almost a hushed voice said, "You were never born into the world of the Earth below. Although you were at one time alive in your mother's womb, you died before you could enter the world on Earth outside your mother's womb. By the grace and mercy of the Lord God Almighty, He brought you back to life here in Paradise Above."

I knew about some of this, for Eric had shared this with me earlier. Yet, I still had questions to be answered, but I had learned that they will be answered in due time. So now even more information was being shared about our being here, as well as those other Rubs.

"These Red-Robed beings are not Rubs!" Eric candidly said, as he continued to speak to us. "There are two separate groups of them. Like you, they are here because of God's grace and mercy. One group is called Ruis, and the other group is called Ruas. Ruis means Redeemed Un-intelligibles, while Ruas means Redeemed Un-accountables." Eric momentarily concluded his speaking and again stepped forward to the table to reclaim his drinking glass, lifted it quickly to his mouth and drained it dry. With a sigh, he put the glass down as he continued with his monologue.

"You see, Ruis and Ruas were alive in their mother's wombs, and were born alive into the world of Earth below. But the Ruis did not have the mental capabilities to know about the Almighty One and their responsibilities regarding Him, so when they died at whatever age on Earth, God brought them home to Paradise Above." Eric explained slowly yet emphatically.

"Now the Ruas are somewhat different. They have the capabilities to know about God and their responsibilities to Him, but are not held accountable for this until they realize their standing before God and what He expects of them. That is why they are called un-accountables, and if they die, for whatever reason, before they individually reach that level, then God will bring them home to Paradise Above," Eric ended with an expiration of breath erupting from his mouth. He took another breath and added, "Also that is why they are here with you in the sessions. They too may learn from the Red-Covered Bible about God."

What a story. I could see that we all were greatly indebted to the Almighty One for this grace and mercy of His. I looked at both Robert and Jeni and wondered if they were thinking the same thing as me. They were silent, but I could see by the expressions on their faces that they had been deeply impressed by what Eric had shared with us.

"Your attention please, your attention please," came a low-sounding authoritative voice from overhead speakers. "The recess is now over, please return to your seats promptly."

The Erics, all three of them, got up and headed for the split-door elevators. Robert, Jeni and I followed closely behind.

CHAPTER 11

Understanding

The session was over. It had been a long one but, entirely worthwhile. After all we learned about Ruis and Ruas, and how we were different from them, but in many ways the same as them. This we knew because of the Almighty One's concern for us as well as for them. Also, every one of them had their own Eric. Surely this was all of God's doing in our behalf.

I had not noticed that as we left the Celestial Academy, that we had departed to our right and out of the massive doors and heading in the opposite direction from which we came. I was too busy contemplating about the Ruis and Ruas responsibilities toward God. Evidently the Ruis had no power of comprehension to know about the Almighty One. Thus, they were not held accountable to Him. But the Ruas, I thought, certainly had the ability to comprehend God. This puzzled me. What then was the reason for them being here? The question kept turning over and over in my mind. Then it came to me that they were very young in their life on Earth, and though they had powers of comprehension, they had not matured to the level of understanding that would make them accountable to God for neither their behavior, nor their acknowledgment of Him as their God. So naturally they, upon their deaths, became Ruas here in Paradise Above.

"That's right, Eric, isn't it?" I blurted out, as we walked along the trail. Everyone stopped abruptly as if we had all walked into an invisible wall.

"What's the matter with you One Fifty-Five?" exclaimed my Eric. "Are you talking to yourself?"

"I apologize for the outburst, but I was thinking that the Ruas must have died at an early age before their comprehension about God had matured to a level of accountability before God," I retorted.

"You know, I was thinking about that also," Jeni admitted.

"Funny, so was I," sounded Robert. "It was on my mind off and on during the session after our recess."

"It looks as if all three of you are thinking in the same vein," volunteered Jeni's Eric. "Look," he began to explain, "those born on Earth are born with an inherent nature of sin, that is to say, they are prone to do things and think things that are contrary to pleasing and honoring God. When they commit acts that are sinful, they need to turn to God for His forgiveness and grace. The young children sin even as older people do, but they are not aware of their sin and of their responsibility to honor God." Eric stated it all rather clearly, I thought, and with that we continued walking along the path.

"So when they die on Earth in that state, they are not held accountable, and thus are given a home in Paradise Above," added Eric as an afterthought.

As we walked along the trail, we could see ourselves with our red and white garments, reflected in the crystal clear river which was flowing in the direction in which we were headed. It had a mesmerizing, yet tranquil, affect upon me, and more than likely on our entire party. For none of us, not even the Erics, had anything to say, for we walked along in the silence of our personal thoughts.

The session after the recess was a vividly impressive one. In my mind's eye, I could see what had transpired upon that magnificent screen. The Hebrews were free now. Yet they spent forty long and difficult years wandering in the wilderness in search of the land which God had promised. He also sustained them with food and drink throughout those years as Moses led them. It appeared at times that they did not appreciate Moses, nor God. They complained and even rebelled. Many were killed by the Lord, for He was greatly disappointed with them. Nevertheless, God dealt with them in compassion. He gave them the Ten Commandments through Moses, His servant. Also, the laws and ordinances by which to live and to serve God were conveyed to Moses for the people. The Tabernacle was established. The Levitical priesthood and the various sacrifices for the forgiveness of sin was put in place for this people. God had raised up a mighty nation for His Glory. Unfortunately, Moses was not allowed to enter into the Promised Land. Joshua, though, received the charge to take the people across the River Jordan into Canaan. Moses died on a mountain overlooking Canaan.

It was an astonishing story. The scenes from that presentation could never be erased from my memory, nor the lessons I gleaned from my viewing. God is an awesome God. His might was wondrous to behold.

One lesson I learned is that man has a sinful way at times, yet at times he practices good things and entertains good thoughts. I also saw that the Almighty One dealt with the people in righteousness and overwhelming compassion.

I was enthralled with the presentation that I had just experienced. So much so, that I was yearning to return to my special place. There I could read again about God's dealings with His chosen people.

This different route we were taking back to our special places was especially beautiful as the trail followed close to the river. The green, towering trees along with the flowers bordering the river reflected brilliant rays of color off the flowing waters. We were walking in luminous colors of light.

"O what beauty," exclaimed Jeni, as her face shone with smiling joy.

At that, we all stopped. We were completely still, breathing in the surrounding splendor of all that was about us.

"It never ceases to amaze me how gorgeous everything is," Robert said enthusiastically as he proceeded to point to everything around us to observe. We really needed a guide to locate these beautiful sights.

"I just don't have the words to express adequately my gratitude to the Almighty One for all that He has created, and for all that He has done for us," Robert proclaimed boldly.

"Yes, you are right," replied his Eric, "even with the Heavenly language we can hardly adequately express our love and gratitude to Him."

"But He knows our hearts," said my Eric. "And that is more than enough for God. He knows us."

"You mean He knows what we think, and how we feel?" I asked, as a newer understanding of the Almighty One began to broaden expand my thinking.

"That's absolutely correct One Fifty-Five," replied my Eric. "He is God. He knows everything."

"That's remarkable," I thought. "What a God we have."

"We need to keep moving," urged Jeni's Eric. "We've been here for awhile."

With that said, we all nodded our heads in agreement and continued on our journey.

Not much was said as we trotted gingerly along the trail, always mindful of the river on our right side with its surrounding landscapes of resplendent beauty. We all knew the river proceeded from the Place of the Almighty One. We Rubs, as far as I could surmise, resided on one side of the river. But what was on the other side of the river? This question was on my mind on more than just one occasion. Just about every time I viewed the river, the question consistently came to mind. Is it another Paradise Above, I wondered, or is it a different place altogether? I knew that Eric had mentioned it. Nevertheless, he had not volunteered any amount of information about it. Perhaps it was a subject that for now was out of bounds.

"Hurry up, One Fifty-Five," I heard, as I looked from the river toward the direction of the voice. It was my Eric calling me. They were far ahead of me, and though I could see them, it was apparent that I had lagged behind, slowed by my thoughts of the river. Evidently, they had just noticed that I was not among them and stopped to call me. I could see my Eric coming quickly toward me. But he was not walking. He was gliding smoothly just a few feet above the trail. Eric arrived and stood in front of me. I could see from the look on his face that he was not too happy. "What have you been doing?" he asked. "Did you not know that you had lagged so far behind us?"

"Eric, I didn't realize that I was so far behind. I kept looking at the river, and wondering what was on the other side. I just lost track of staying up with you," I sheepishly explained. "I'm sorry, I'll hurry up."

"That won't be fast enough," replied Eric. "Here hop on my back," he commanded, as he turned looking toward the others far down the road.

I hesitated at the mention of getting on his back. I wasn't sure what he had planned.

"Come on. What are you waiting for? We are just going to catch up with them."

At that I jumped on his back, straddled my legs around his waist while grasping his shoulders with my hands. No sooner was I in place when we took off a few feet above the ground, and almost instantly arrived at the place where Robert, Jeni, and the Erics were waiting.

"What happened to you?" questioned Robert, as I climbed off Eric's back. "We were just walking along at a good pace and suddenly Jeni wondered where you were. Then we all noticed that you were not with us. There you were way down the trail. What happened?" he repeated.

"I told Eric," I responded. "I'm sorry for the delay. I just kept thinking about the river and what was on the other side, and I guess it just slowed me down."

"Well, you are here now," interrupted Jeni's Eric. "Let's continue on our way to your special places. We are almost there," he urged us, as he waved his arm and pointed up the trail which prompted all of us to walk again.

No sooner had we traveled a short distance, than I noticed just ahead of us and along our side of the river, a towering white building just beyond the trees in the distance. Jeni, Robert, and I had walked ahead of our Erics, who were talking amongst themselves oblivious to our being now ahead of them. Jeni must have seen the building the same time that I observed it, for she grabbed my arm, causing me and Robert to stop.

"What is that?" she cried aloud.

"Don't ask me," I replied. "I have no idea. It cannot be the Celestial Academy, we just left it."

By now Robert also noticed the building, for we had all stopped to gaze at this large structure appearing above the trees just to the front of us. "That's right," Robert affirmed, "it is definitely not the academy. Perhaps it is another academy that we know nothing about."

"We only know about one building," I reminded them as a matter of fact. "This is something new," I surmised, which, of course, was obvious to all of us. We had no other idea of what the building might be. Our best collected guess was that it was another academy. It was big. It was white, and if it was bigger than what it appears from where we were standing then it must be very similar to the building which we had recently left.

Just then the three Erics arrived. They were still talking. I was puzzled by what they had to talk about, but then they had so much more information about everything than what we had. Plus, I believe that they talked about us, comparing their notes. After all they are our Erics. We all know that they are genuinely concerned about us.

"No, One Fifty-Five, Robert, and Jeni. This is not an academy," my Eric exclaimed. "Let's just keep walking. We will be passing the building soon then we will stop there to look at it," he promised.

"But what is this building, Eric?" I asked, almost pleadingly.

"Yes, tell us," Jeni chimed in.

"Be patient," Eric chided. "When we get there we will tell you about this building," he again promised us.

"Well then let's go," urged Robert.

There was nothing left to talk about. It was apparent that we needed to travel immediately to that building beyond the trees. We were eager to do because we were all determined to arrive there as quickly as possible. So, off we went.

It seemed as if we would never arrive. The building loomed in front of us only a short distance away, yet it appeared that we were making little progress, even though we were walking much faster than before. I kept thinking, what can this building be if it is not another academy? My anticipation was getting the best of me. I wanted to get there right away so that Eric could tell us about this large structure. "Would we be able to go into it?" I thought. 'What's inside and why have we never noticed the building before?' It's next to the river, yet until just recently, we have never seen it.

"What do you think it really is?" asked Robert as he whispered in my ear.

"I still don't know Robert. We've been through this before," I quietly but emphatically reminded him, as we kept on walking. I could see that Jeni was smiling happily as she continued to fix her attention on the building ahead. Did she anticipate something that would make her smile so? Perhaps she knew something that Robert and I did not know. That couldn't be. I was sure. She smiles a lot anyway, I began to notice. Maybe all the female human being Rubs smiled a lot. It could be their very nature. I didn't know for sure, but Jeni was a smiler, that was certain.

Finally, we arrived at the building. The road became broader just before we arrived, which gave us a fuller perspective of the size of the structure. It was no academy. It was larger, by far, than the Celestial Academy with which we were familiar. The building is so immense that I now realized that when we first noticed it, that it appeared to be ever so close because it was so big. But of course, it was farther away then we calculated. We all breathed a sigh of relief. Nevertheless, we were filled with great awe as we stood looking up toward the top of the building. There over the massive, double, golden doors, shinning forth from the alabaster white structure, was the building's name. It was spelled out in sparkling, large golden letters, The Alpha and Omega Celestial Library.

"Well, are you all happy?" asked Roberts Eric.

"Now you can see for yourselves that this is a library," added Jeni's Eric.

"I don't know what a library is, but it is surely impressive," volunteered Jeni. Still smiling she stated, "it's taller than all these trees, and must be at least twice the size of the Celestial Academy."

"Right you are Jeni," replied my Eric. "It is larger than the hall, but for a good reason. You see, a library is where writings and records are stored. Writings as in the Red-Covered Book, records of writings, and even visual recordings like those you saw in the Celestial Academy."

"Why is the library so large?" asked Jeni with a look of amazement.

I didn't ask, but was wondering the same thing. 'How big are these writings and recordings that are stored there? Is that why the library is so immense so as to accommodate them?' These were questions racing through my mind and as I was about to voice them to Eric, any Eric, my Eric answered, "You see the words Alpha and Omega?" he asked us.

"Yes," we all replied accompanied by the nodding of our collective heads.

"Alpha means beginning, while Omega means the ending or the end," stated Eric. "Everything that has ever been done, or will ever be done by the Almighty One with all His creation and creatures, is stored in both written and visual records in this library of the Lord's. As you will soon read in your Red Bibles in the Gospel of John, John declares 'that there are also many other things which Jesus did, the which, if they should be written everyone, I suppose that even the world itself could not contain the books that should be written,'" concluded Eric.

"You're looking at the building that houses all of these," added Robert's Eric. "And, even more," he confided, "the records of the lives of all human beings and spirit beings that have ever lived are stored in the Celestial Library."

"Do all three of you remember when God said in Genesis 'let us make man in our image'?" asked Jeni's Eric.

"Certainly," I replied, "how could anyone forget that? Seeing God mold man out of the dust of the ground and breathing the breath of life into him, creating a living being. Who could ever forget that?" I redundantly repeated.

"Well, One Fifty-Five, Robert, and Jeni, the Almighty One, Jesus, and the Holy Spirit are all one, yet they at times are revealed separately as the Father, the Son, and the Holy Spirit. It is in Their collective Image that man was created long ago," continued Jeni's Eric.

"It is all in the Book, and in the Celestial Library, which by the way, is available to those who want to further enhance their study of the Scriptures in their Red-Covered Bible," added Robert's Eric, as he focused our attention to the massive, golden doors of the Alpha and Omega Celestial Library.

"Can we go in now and look around?" Jeni asked, as she strode toward the doors of the library.

"Wait a minute, Jeni," yelled her Eric. "Not today! Some other time. We need to get all of you back to your special places."

"But…" Robert blurted.

"No," interrupted Robert's Eric, "we can do this another time. In fact, you can visit on your own, when you have the time," he explained.

"We do not know how to use the library," I offered, hoping that they would take us in and educate us personally on the proper use of the Celestial Library.

It didn't work. My Eric quickly replied, "all the instructions are listed inside on a large screen for all to see. Now let's just get going," he urged. "You need to be in your own individual space, and continue your readings in the Red-Covered Bible from Joshua all the way through the Old Testament."

"That's a lot of reading to accomplish before the next session," challenged Jeni's Eric, as he gently led her away from the golden doors down the trail to our special places.

The rest of us followed behind. Now I was more eager than ever to arrive at my own place and, to study again the Book in my leisure area, and to attend to my beautiful special place.

As we followed Jeni and her Eric, I took one backward glance at that gleaming alabaster library, and wondered if there were some secrets there to be discovered. I recall that it was said that the records of all those that lived are stored there. What an astounding fact.

CHAPTER 12

Curious

I knew it would feel good to be in my special place again. But upon my arrival, it was better than I had anticipated. All was in place. Nothing really had changed except, there appeared to be more fruit upon the trees. I sauntered over to the lounge area, plucked a few luscious-looking fruits to eat, and sat down in my chair, absolutely thrilled to be back.

After taking a few bites of one of the tasty fruits, I opened my Red-Covered Bible and turned to Joshua. I remembered Eric said to continue my reading from there through the Old Testament. That was certainly a lot of Bible to read, let alone to be able to comprehend. But recently I noticed that I could read much more rapidly now than when I first began.

My understanding also was greatly enhanced. No doubt, I thought, this has to be the Almighty One's influence upon my personal abilities, and His Spirit being present.

Joshua took over from Moses, as he campaigned across Jordan into Canaan, the Promised Land. He was victorious in his military campaigns that were largely responsible for bringing the Israelites into a land, and forming a nation composed of the Twelve Tribes. Two notable things, I believe, that occurred during Joshua's time of leadership was the battle of Jericho, in which the walls of the walled city fell down completely flat, at the sound of the trumpets and the shout of the people as they encircled the city. The other remarkable occurrence was when the sun itself, "stood still in the midst of Heaven." This enabled the army of Joshua to be victorious over the confederation of the Amorites.

My reading was moving swiftly. I was learning so much about God and His dealings with His people. Beside that, as I continued to read, I felt as if I was there myself, as if I was sitting in the Celestial Academy and viewing all of Joshua's and the Israelites' experiences first hand. This will probably happen, I thought, when we attend the next session. We will see all that we have been reading about on that immense screen. Hopefully we will see Joshua himself.

I turned to Judges, somewhat saddened by reading of Joshua's death. Moses was dead and now Joshua. Who will lead these people? I soon found out that God had a plan for them, but they did not always listen and follow Him, even though He raised up a number of judges to lead and rule as His representatives. As I finished reading Judges, I was wondering why the people had such a difficult time in their lives. If they had only followed God, all would have been well. They would have prospered, but it was not so. With them it seemed like a repeated occurrence. They would have fellowship with God on a national scale, then they would turn from Him and fall into apostasy. Next they would fall into captivity. Later they would repent of their sins toward God, and cry unto Him for deliverance. Then God would deliver them through the leadership of a number of judges that He raised up for that very purpose.

There were so many of those judges. Othniel; Ehud; Shamgar; Deborah; Barak; Gideon; Abimelech; Tola; Jair; Jeophthah; Ibzan; Elon; Abdon; and Samson were all chosen of God to deliver the Israelites from bondage. Yet with all of the heroes of God in the end, after Samson's death, the people had no leader to rule over them. Consequently, as I finished my readings in Judges, there was this ending statement: "In those days there was no king in Israel: every man did that which was right in his own sight."

How strange it was that these chosen and favored people of God kept rebelling against Him. What was wrong with them? I asked myself. Then I remembered what Eric had said about those humans on Earth. They were capable of sin. Perhaps, I mused, sin could lead them away from God.

"You look like you are in deep thought," spoke a familiar voice from behind me. I knew instantly that it was Jeni. I turned in my lounge chair to see her approaching me from just beyond the trail leading to my space.

"Yes, Jeni, what are you doing here?" I asked. "And, yes, I've just finished reading Judges and have been thinking about it."

"Well, now that you have asked," she said with a smile, "I've come over to share from my readings in Ruth," as she pointed to her Red-Covered Bible that she held in her raised hand. "I thought it would be a good thing if you heard about Ruth from a female Rub's view," she declared emphatically.

"Here, sit here, Jeni," I requested, as I motioned to her to sit in a chair that was adjacent to mine.

"Thanks One Fifty-Five, I was hoping you'd be glad to see me, and even be open to me sharing Ruth with you," she responded with a semi laugh.

As she sat down, I noticed her eyes were gleaming with excitement. She must have been really affected by her readings of Ruth, I surmised. "I'm all yours Jeni," I assured her. "Please tell me about Ruth, I haven't read that portion of the Bible yet."

That was all she needed. She opened her Bible, scooted back deeper into the chair, adjusted her Rub's robe, began to talk about the Book of Ruth, and to summarize what she had read.

Evidently Naomi, a Jewess, left her native land with her husband and two sons to live in the land of the Moabites during the Israeli time of the Judges. Naomi's husband died. Her two sons married women of Moab. One was named Ruth and the other Orpah. Unfortunately both of Naomi's sons died, leaving her with two daughters-in-law. Naomi decided to return to her own land and people, she told the two widowed wives to return to their mother's house. Oprah went, but Ruth stayed with Naomi, pledging that Naomi's people should be her people, and Naomi's God should be her God.

The more thrilling and beautiful part of the story takes place as they return to Naomi's land. There they are well received. Boaz, a kinsman of Naomi's husband, redeem, not only her property, according to Jewish law, but takes Ruth as his wife to complete the obligations of the kinsman-redeemer. Boaz and Ruth have a son born unto them named Obed, who later becomes the progenitor of King David.

Jeni laid her Bible on the table, stood up, adjusted her robe, then sat back in her chair. She had finished sharing with me her readings in Ruth.

"Thank you Jeni, I really enjoyed that. I appreciate you telling me about Naomi, Ruth, and Boaz. It is an inspiring story," I said.

"You are more than welcome," she replied graciously. "It was a privilege to share the Book of Ruth with you." At that she rose up quickly and began to explore my place as she sauntered toward her place.

Both Jeni and I did not know it at that time, but we later learned that Ruth, Boaz, and King David were all in the lineage of Jesus the Christ, God's Son, who would be born into the world in the years to come. When He came, He would deal with the sins of men forever.

Try as I may the past conversation with Eric about my 'demise' kept creeping back into my thoughts. I supposed it was true also with Robert and 003. There remained a lot of questions regarding this and I wondered if I would ever become acquainted with what happened on Earth.

The thought left me quickly, as I was remembering my Eric telling me of the next session at the Academy was soon. It would be covering our assignments to read after Ruth and then on to Isaiah. I looked into the front of the Bible where the contents listed all of its books. I could see there was a lot of reading before me, as well as many future sessions to attend.

"Well, I know about Ruth thanks to Jeni," I thought. I began to read First Samuel.

Hearing some noise, I looked up and a smiling Jeni stood in front of me eating a fruit.

"Look One Fifty-Five I'm sorry to bother you," Jeni said sheepishly, "but I must talk to you."

I closed my Bible, put it on the adjacent table, looked up at Jeni and said, "pull up a chair and let's talk. Now what's so urgent?"

"Well," replied Jeni, as she adjusted her position in the chair, leaned forward and whispered, "I'm so curious about what happened to me down below," she paused. "I keep thinking about it."

"Me too," I admitted. "It's often in my thoughts." I assured her.

"Do you think Robert is bothered by this also," she asked.

"If we are and he isn't, then something is wrong with us or him," I expressed, a little louder than I had planned.

"Not so loud," advised Jeni, "You know our Erics are always around," she whispered.

There was some silence now. We both sat back in our chairs contemplating.

"Look," I blurted out. "The Erics would not have let us know or even taken us to the Celestial Library if they did not want us to know about ourselves and what happened on Earth. Isn't that right?" I questioned excitedly.

Jeni sat up in her chair, looked me in the eye and said, "I think you are right One-Fifty Five."

"What about Robert?" I asked.

"Let's go talk to him, okay?" replied Jeni.

"Hey," came a familiar voice, "what are you two up to?" asked Robert as he approached both Zero Zero Five and me from behind a few trees. He too was munching on some of the delicious fruit in my garden.

We were startled as well as surprised, for we both thought it was one of our Erics until we recognized Roberts voice.

"You guys up to something?" asked Robert. "You both look almost guilty of plotting something," he added with a mischievous grin.

"Well we are plotting, but we are not guilty," responded Jeni somewhat defiantly. "We were just coming over to your place to see if you would like to join us in this plot of ours."

"I'm all ears," responded Robert, as he pulled up a nearby chair and scooted it over to where we were sitting. He sat down with a sigh, while still eating and talking through the whole process. "Well, what is it that seems to be so secretive?" he ventured, looking to Jeni and then to me.

"It's about down below, and all that," offered One Fifty-Five.

"You mean the killings?" asked Robert.

"How did you know?" asked the surprised Jeni.

"Just a thought, I guess," pronounced Robert, "I've had that subject on my mind ever since we visited the Celestial Library." Robert paused, cleared his throat, and continued, "why did the Erics even take us there? Was there a reason for it?" He paused again, got up from the chair, looked around, and said, "the Erics want us to know about our killings, there is no doubt about it. I'm convinced that it is so," he said affirmatively while sitting back down.

"That's it then," summarized Jeni. "It sounds like you are with us Robert," as she addressed Robert with a questioning look.

"Count me in, most assuredly," he insisted. "Now what's the plan?"

"Haven't got that far yet, but we've got to get to the library before any of this will happen," I stated.

We all nodded our heads in agreement. Now we needed to formulate a plan.

Well, it wasn't much of a plan, we all agreed. It was as simple as one, two, and three. Get going early in the morning to the Celestial Library, and then go from there. We certainly were not going to call our Erics for this venture. It was a Rub-only event.

Step one had been completed. We were now in the Celestial Library. But, what to do for step two or even three was still to be determined.

"I think we need to go to the auditorium," offered Robert.

"That's a good start," agreed Jeni.

"Yeah," I countered. "What do we do when we get there?" I asked skeptically.

"Do you suggest we go anywhere else first?" countered Robert. "While we are here in this grand entry mall there must be some signs or directions on how to get around," he continued as he began slowly to survey their surroundings.

Robert and Jeni conceded, thinking that would be a prudent thing to do. So they proceeded to follow me as I made my way through the area.

I stopped at a place on the nearby wall. There was block or something that looked like a rectangular slab protruding from the wall. We all stopped there to look at it, but were thoroughly puzzled because it was blank, all of it, nothing was on it.

"What is this?" exclaimed Jeni.

"Who knows?" supported Robert.

"It's got to be something though," I pondered. "It's here for a reason, don't you think?" I questioned.

"Look there's a button on the wall next to that block," Jeni blurted out. "Right there at the lower left beside that block," she described it, pointing to it with her extended finger.

"You're closer, Robert, push it," she said as she urged him.

"Well, okay," replied Robert, "here goes."

At that he pushed the button, and lo and behold, the whole block lit up. It was a directional information board. It was in alphabetical order, with title and subjects, and where to go in the library to locate them. Starting at A was Adam: Creation room-North Hall. On and on the topics went. But the one that got all of our attention was the B...Below-History-Celestial Auditorium. That had to be it. We all agreed. But where was the auditorium? 'The Erics had taken us there earlier,' thought Jeni, but now she was not sure which hallway they should take.

"Press the button again Robert," pleaded Jeni. The screening light ceased.

The screen lit up, and promptly Jeni ran her finger over Below-History-Celestial Auditorium and a green light appeared.

"That's it," she declared, "We take the green hallway to the Celestial Auditorium."

We looked at all the hallways that proceeded out of the grand entry way and saw no overhead lights. It was rather disheartening, but we had failed to look on the floor.

"Look there, the green light over to your right," I yelled. "Right there on the floor in front of the entrance to that hallway!" I said as I quickly walked over to it. Both Robert and Jeni hurriedly followed. We entered the green hall way. We were off to the Celestial Auditorium.

We soon entered into a lavishly, green-decorated auditorium with rows of green, plush seats. No one was there but us. Perhaps we had picked the right time to come.

"Now that we are here," stated Robert, "what should we do?" he questioned.

"I'm not sure," I replied.

"Let's sit down here in the front row," suggested Jeni, "look around, get our bearings, and go from there," she pleaded.

"Well, okay, no one offered any other idea," replied Robert, as all three of us walked to the center of the front row seats, sat down staring at the large screen before us.

"Will you believe this?" uttered Robert, "right here on the arm rests are the menus for the screen."

Upon saying that, he pressed the on-off button. The massive screen lit up with a visible menu displayed. Again as in the grand entry way, many choices appeared. They saw history as the choice they wanted to select, and were directed to push the H button on the arm rest.

"You do it, Robert, you started this," I insisted.

Robert pushed the button. The menu appeared with a long list of choices from general history to Bible history listed A through Z. But the one listed 'personal' caught our attention.

"Push that one," urged Jeni.

Robert was now completely fascinated by this whole setting, not to mention the screen with all of its listings.

"What are you waiting for Robert? Just push personal," Jeni added, her voice expressing urgency.

Robert, seemingly awakening from his momentary distraction, looked for the button marked H and pushed hard, as if that would have had some affect upon the screen and its menu. The menu on the screen read: *Enter name or number or both from the selections on your arm rest.*

We were all caught up in this extraordinary moment. At the touch of a finger, anticipated things would be see on this screen, right before our eyes. It was unknown, but each one of us was sure it would be about him and his history on Earth.

A silence pervaded the auditorium. No one spoke. It was as if we were frozen in our own thoughts. Do we really want to step out into the unknown? Each one, Robert, Jeni and I unsurprisingly shared this same thought. Yet, the compulsion to know about our killings outweighed all. We must know.

"You're first, One Fifty-Five, enter your number, don't be timid," challenged Jeni.

I shook my head in approval, and slowly entered the number: 31,683,155. The light in the auditorium slowly faded. The screen disappeared, and there was resurrected an Earthly scene.

BOOK II

Earth and Heaven

CHAPTER 13

Jerusha

"Jerusha."

"Yes, Mom," Jerusha replied, "what do you want?"

"Do you know what time it is?" asked Rachael. Jerusha's mother, Rachael, seemed somewhat impatient. You could hear it in the tone of her voice. If Jerusha could see her in the other room, opposite her bedroom, she would know by looking at her mother's face that she displayed some obvious misgivings.

Rachael was young-looking beyond her years. After bearing three children, of which Jerusha was the oldest, she still appeared as young as an upper-college student. Though she was a bit larger now, after her child bearing, her figure remained attractive to the eye. One could also see that she was mindful of her body, for she gave the appearance of being quite fit. Her shoulder length black hair, which glistened in the late afternoon light, encompassed a face that was strikingly beautiful.

"No, Mom, I've lost all track of time," answered Jerusha, frankly.

"Well, it's getting late. Don't you want to be on time! Doesn't the banquet begin at 7? What time is Ryan supposed to pick you up?" yelled Rachael from across the hall.

Jerusha was attempting frantically to get ready for the big high school graduation banquet. She hesitated to answer her mother, thinking 'she knows the answers to all those questions. We've talked about them for days. She just wants to hurry me. She's a stickler for promptness.' "Okay Mother! I get the message," Jerusha called back assuredly, "everything will be just fine."

Just then the doorbell rang. Someone was at the front door. Rachael looked out from the upstairs bedroom window to see who it was, but the palm tree beside the house hid the person or people from her view. The bell rang again, but longer this time, prompting Rachael go quickly to the hall and yell. "Is anybody down there? Dad can you get the door. Didn't you hear the bell ring?"

"Hold your horse's honey," a calm voice replied from the den on the lower floor. "I'll get it."

"Well okay," she responded with a sigh, "but don't keep them waiting, whoever they are."

Jacob made a few clicks on the mouse, got up from his straight back computer chair, pushed it aside, and headed for the front door. He moved quickly, even though he was a large man, to the front door. He looked to see who was there. Again the door bell rang. He opened the door.

He could see right away that it was a delivery man. He also spotted the delivery van at the curb with the name Westside Florist displayed on the vehicle's panel. "Now what could he want?" Jacob thought.

"Is this the Goldenstein residence?" asked the short, blond-haired youth standing awkwardly before him.

"Why yes, it is," answered Jacob, now remembering that his daughter Jerusha had a big day on her calendar today.

"Is there a Jerusha Goldenstein here," asked the youth hurriedly.

"Yes, she lives here."

"Well, this corsage is for her," he stated, as he held out a ribbon-wrapped box. "Can you sign for it?"

"Certainly." Jacob took the clipboard, signed the paper, took the box, returned the clipboard, politely thanked the boy, and said goodbye as he quickly closed the door.

Rachael heard the door close. She thought she heard a car door slam, and a car drive away from the curb. "Well, what is it?" she inquired somewhat impatiently, as she stepped out into the hall.

"It's for Jerusha. A corsage or something, I guess, for this evening's activities," he replied. "It's probably from Ronnie, the guy Jerusha is dating," he added.

"Bring it up here, will you? So I can pin it on her. She should be ready. Her date will arrive any minute now," Rachael stated with an assuring voice. Quickly she reminded Jacob that his name was Ryan, not Ronnie, and cautioned her husband not to embarrass the boy.

No sooner had Jacob rushed upstairs with the corsage and was in the process of opening the box to give it to Rachael, when the doorbell rang again, not once, but three times, in rapid succession. No doubt it was Ryan. From the sounds of the ringing doorbell, it appeared that he was in a jovial but somewhat boyish mood.

"Oh!" exclaimed Jerusha, "that must be Ryan!"

"Jacob would you mind opening the door and inviting him in? My hands are full," pleaded Rachael. "Jerusha will be down in a few minutes. Keep him entertained, won't you? Please?" She implored.

"Okay," replied Jacob. What else could he say or do he thought, as he descended the stairs. Jacob never cared much for Ronnie or Ryan, whatever his name. He was handsome enough, with broad shoulders and a firm build, but Jacob still had reservations about him since he and Jerusha started their occasional dating just a few months ago. Ryan was also the star running back on the local high school football team.

Ryan Ortega was not a Jew. That was strike number one. Although they had invited him to attend the synagogue with them he had chosen not to go. That was strike number two. Ryan was a Catholic, as he proudly declared, but not a very faithful one.

Jacob found out that Ryan was the only son of his Hispanic dad. His mother was Caucasian. This, he thought, probably is why Ryan has black hair and a darker complexion. Nevertheless, Ryan had a winsome smile, which beamed below his piercing, brown eyes. Jacob could see why Jerusha might be attracted to him. Nevertheless, Jacob was not for this match with his daughter. This could be strike number three. They were going off to college soon, he thought, and this casual relationship will fade. Jerusha should only date Jewish boys, but he had made an exception with Ryan so as not to appear too dogmatic in their faith. Recently Jerusha had displayed some intermittent signs of rebellion regarding their faith, and Jacob wanted to deal gently with her attitude. Most of all, he did not want to alienate her from their faith by being overbearing.

Jacob opened the door. Ryan stood there dressed in a black tux with a red bow tie protruding beneath his square-jawed chin. He looked absolutely manly, thought Jacob. If only he were a Jew, or at least if he would even consider converting to Judiasm. Oh well, the fanciful wish quickly faded as he greeted Ryan.

"Good evening, Mr. Goldenstein," said a smiling Ryan. "How are you tonight?"

"Just fine."

"You look great Ryan. Come on in, Jerusha should be down shortly." Jacob closed the door, and motioned Ryan to follow him into the living room. "Have a seat," as he pointed to the chair opposite his chair.

No sooner had they sat down, when Jerusha, followed by her mother burst into the room. Both Jacob and Ryan stood quickly and looked toward the two women who were approaching them. Seeing them side by side, if Ryan had not known any better, he would have mistaken Jerusha and Rachael for twin sisters.

Jerusha was radiant. She was as close to being the 'spitting image' of her mother as possible. Her face was glowing, with her black hair cascading down onto her bare shoulders.

She was an exceptional beauty. Her soft, dark eyes and ruby-like lips only amplified the total loveliness of her face. She was slender. More so than Rachael, yet her figure displayed the leanness and agility that she had acquired from years of training as a cheerleader.

The orchid corsage from Ryan was pinned just below her left shoulder, and adorned the full-flowing knee-length, softly-colored yellow, gown she was wearing.

Jacob was tongue tied. His little girl was a woman. 'She is absolutely beautiful,' he thought.

"Good to see you Ryan," Rachael said, as she took Jerusha's hand and spun her around for all to see. "Well, how does your date look?" she asked proudly.

"She's a definite knockout, Mrs. Goldenstein," he said, as he strode a few steps toward Jerusha and said to her, "You look great, are we ready to go?"

Jerusha didn't answer, but gave him a knowing nod as if to say yes. Then still, radiant and smiling, she took Ryan's hand and spun him around for all to see and said, "Well, how does my date look?" They all started laughing. It was funny. Jerusha definitely had a sense of humor.

"He looks absolutely splendid," responded Rachael. "You two are a knockout couple," she exclaimed.

"That's for sure," Jacob affirmed.

"Have a terrific evening, the both of you," said Rachael.

"And," added Jacob seriously, "don't forget your coming home time, okay Ryan?"

"Yes sir, will do," replied Ryan. "Goodnight, Mr. and Mrs. Goldenstein," he said, looking back as he and Jerusha left the room. Hand in hand they departed through the front door.

CHAPTER 14

The Banquet

The Lake Land County High School graduation banquet was a gala event. Every senior looked forward to it eagerly each spring. This spring was no exception. The banquet was being held downtown in the elite Victorian Hotel that had been rented for this special occasion. It was a traditional site. The hotel was one of those rare buildings that had withstood the onslaught of time and served, since day one, as the place for the senior banquet of Lake Land Country High School.

"This place is beautiful, isn't it?" asked Jerusha as she looked around excitedly.

"Sure is," responded Ryan. "This is your first time here, is that right?"

"Yes, I could have come last year, but my folks said no. This is really special, its more than I had heard about, I mean so beautiful and all."

They parked the car in the parking garage across the street and took the elevator down to street level. Just as they crossed the street, a light rain began to fall, forcing them to walk quickly toward the hotel entrance. They entered through the glass revolving door into a crowded lobby full of excited young people dressed in formal attire.

Strains of music could be heard as they made their way to the giant ballroom down the hall.

"Hi Jerusha. Hey Ryan," greeted some classmates as they sauntered by the couple.

"Hi yourself," they replied. "See you in the ballroom," they yelled back, as they continued down the hallway.

Ryan still had a hold of Jerusha's hand, and started to lead her through the crowd of people toward the ballroom. For some reason, she was not following him, but kept stopping every few strides. Ryan looked back at her and started to ask what was wrong, when he noticed her looking up toward the ceiling. He paused and gazed upward also. 'So that was it,' he realized. She was staring at the immense glass, chandelier hanging above them.

"Isn't that one of the most beautiful chandeliers you have ever seen?" she asked.

"It is beautiful and bright, but we need to get to our seats at the table. It's getting late," he urged her as he led their way down the hall into the grand ballroom.

They entered the dimly-lit ballroom, looking for their table with their names on the place settings. They located them quickly, and noticed they were seated at one of the tables closest to the head table. The band was still playing softly as others found their respective seats also. Jerusha again looked up as she sat down and exclaimed, "Ryan, look at that giant ball hanging from the ceiling. That's really something."

Ryan noticed it also. The silver-mirrored ball was spinning slowly, and scattering beams of colored light across the expansive room. "Man, that's pretty sharp," agreed Ryan. "The table and everything is really impressive," he said, as he continued to look about the room with a startled gaze.

"Looks like everyone is here," stated Jerusha, as she waved to her friends seated at other tables. They in turn smiled and waved back.

"Yeah, look. There are some of the cheerleaders with their dates," Ryan said, as he nudged her and pointed to the table where they were seated.

"Ryan, I see some of your teammates over there on the other side of the room. Look see, right there near the bandstand. Why aren't we seated at their tables?" she asked randomly.

Ryan stared at her with an unbelieving look. "Don't you remember you wanted to be somewhat away from the cheerleaders and the football players," he said sharply. "We requested that. Have you changed your mind now?"

"Oh, no, Ryan, forgive me, I didn't mean that. This is just perfect," she replied rather sheepishly.

"Well okay," Ryan said quickly, as he was ready to move on to something else.

In their conversation and excitement of being at the banquet, they did not notice the two empty seats across the table from them. Evidently their dinner partners were late or perhaps not coming at all. Ryan reached over the table and tilted the name tags towards him so as to be able to read them.

The one tag read 'Jake Bronski,' and the other read 'Melissa Moody.' Jake was the starting linebacker on their football team, and Melissa was one of the players on the girl's soccer team. 'What a combination,' thought Ryan. Jake is supposed to stop the run and now he is dating a gal that's always on the run. The thought amused him. So he shared it with Jerusha who thought it was rather funny also.

Jerusha remarked, "I guess they came to some kind of impasse, for they are not here."

"Perhaps it's the rain," Ryan remarked. "Remember it started just as we came in."

"Yes," murmured Jerusha. She was hoping they wouldn't show, as she had never cared much for Jake. Somehow he gave her the creeps. There was something about him, she could not put her finger on it though. He just seemed strange at times, like he was two different people. She did not know Melissa very well, only casually. She wondered why she was Jake's date for this occasion.

The band had concluded their prelude music for the audience so as to allow the master of ceremonies to make the usual welcoming announcements common to these kinds of occasions. No sooner had the man stood up to talk, then in comes Jake and Melissa through the side exit door. Jerusha could see them. They looked hurried and somewhat bewildered. Jerusha wondered why they were coming in through an exit. They must have not come into the building by the main entrance she concluded.

Jerusha tugged on Ryan's coat sleeve. He was glued to the speaker, and did not see his buddy Jake and his date at the exit door.

"Ryan, look over there," Jerusha said, as she pointed toward the couple.

"It's Jake and Melissa," declared Ryan.

"I know that," she retorted. "Wave at them, won't you?" Jerusha asked. "They are looking for their table."

Ryan stood up, quickly waved arms over his head so as to be noticed. Jake picked up the signal, looked to his date, and then pointed to Ryan as they proceeded toward their table.

They caused a slight commotion, as Jake weaved his way around tables while dragging Melissa behind him. It appeared as if he was in a football game, and that he was approaching a runner to make a tackle as swiftly as possible. Poor Melissa stumbled behind. Ryan and Jerusha watched them make their way through the ballroom.

The master of ceremonies had completed his comments, but neither Ryan nor Jerusha heard a word of it. The band began to play again and waiters appeared, as if out of nowhere, with trays of food and began serving the guests. Jake and Melissa arrived at their table, somewhat out of breath, but ahead of the waiters.

"Hey, guys," snorted Jake, "this is Melissa. You know Ryan, don't you?" he asked.

"Yes, hi Ryan," she responded cheerfully.

Ryan saw the waiter approaching behind them with his tray of food. "Jake," he said interrupting the introductions, "you and Melissa need to sit down. The waiters are coming,"

"Okay," responded Jake, as he and Melissa quickly took their seats. No sooner had they seated themselves when the waiter placed their food in front of them.

"Melissa, you know Jerusha too, don't you?" asked Jake, as he attempted to complete the introductions.

"Jake, we all know each other," interjected Jerusha. "We don't have to go through this. "Isn't that right Melissa?" she queried.

"Sure is," she agreed still smiling.

Ryan asked, "Where have you guys been?"

There was a pause in the conversation as both Jake and Melissa looked at each other to see who would answer Ryan's question. Melissa, usually not a very talkative person, volunteered the information, much to the surprise of Jake. "Well, you see," she began, "when Jake picked me up at the house, it began to rain. Just lightly at first, but it got heavier on our way over there," she signed, caught her breath and continued. "But we ran into a traffic jam."

"Yeah," interrupted Jake. "Some car slid into another one on the slick pavement. That sort of messed us up," he concluded with raised hands.

"We had to take another route," added Melissa.

"So it was late when we got here, and we didn't want to come in to the ballroom through the front door," Jake explained, again gesturing with raised hands.

"So that's why you came in the side exit," Ryan said, with that matter-of-fact look on his face that Jerusha did not particularly like.

"Exactly," stated Jake. "The doorman told us how to get to that exit. Luckily it was not locked."

"Look, we better start eating. We are a little behind everyone else," chimed in Jerusha.

At the remark, the two couples quietly began eating their meals. The food was very tasty, and they spent the next few minutes enthusiastically enjoying the scrumptious meal.

The music from the band softly permeated the large room. The main lights had been dimmed, giving the affair a subtle atmosphere which appeared to have an overall effect upon the guests. Their table talk became more subdued while the task of eating the meal, for the most of them, appeared to be their primary activity.

The master of ceremonies cleared the air as he began to gently tap his half-full water glass. Those seated near the head table instantly responded to him but it took awhile for the other guests in the far part of the room to give him their attention.

"Ladies and gentleman, honored guests, and friends," he announced while raising his voice, and waving his hand towards all the seated guests. "We are doing things a bit different tonight," he paused, straightened his tie, and picked up a program from the table. "As you can see from your program the next thing on the agenda will be your invitation to enjoy this marvelous band and kick up your heels on the dance floor."

At that a number of couples began to leave their tables and head for the dance floor. The band's music became more amplified, and the conversation levels among the guests became noisier. Ryan looked at Jerusha and was about to escort her to the floor, when the master of ceremonies asked for everyone to remain still and quiet for a moment. The band master picked up the queue from the speaker, and quickly quieted the band.

"I apologize," he said hastily, "I didn't finish what I was planning to announce. Please bear with me. This is important. After our dancing time, we would request that the guests would be seated at their tables for dessert, which will be followed by the Awards Ceremony. Please enjoy the rest of the evening," he added, as he returned to his seat.

It did not take long before the dance floor became jam-packed. The band returned to its swing mode, and the people at the head table remained seated. It appeared that they were enjoying the whole scene before them.

Ryan and Jerusha made it to the dance floor and meshed into the crowd. Jake was not much of a dancer, so he sat out while Ryan danced on and off with Jerusha and Melissa. Finally, Jake decided to try some time on the floor with Melissa, and he seemed to be doing okay. There really was not enough space on the floor for fancy dancing, which was okay by Jake. Couples were crowded together, and the whole mass of young people swayed, almost in concert, with the music.

Jerusha enjoyed her dancing with Ryan. They were very close, and their bodies pressed against each other as they moved through the crowded floor. She had not danced quite like this before, and especially with one like Ryan, whom she really liked. She began to experience some emotions that were new to her. They felt good. She had this intense desire to release herself to the mood of the moment, yet she had some disturbing misgivings in her mind. Ryan pressed her closer to him and cuddled her neck. She could feel his warm breath on her neck as he continued to hold her tightly. Her heart began to beat faster. She felt a warm rush all over her body. Ryan did not say a word. They were not looking at one another as when they first began to dance, but were now in a tight embrace. Their dancing had come to a standstill. They remained motionless, barely swaying with the music, completely unaware of anyone else's presence on the dance floor. They were in a world of their own.

"Would you look at the clinging love birds," joked Jake, as he and Melissa danced by them. "Come on you guys, it's time for tables and dessert," he grumbled. "I'm hungry, and so is Melissa. Come join us," he blurted, almost like a command.

Jerusha was a bit flushed, and deeply embarrassed to be caught in that situation. She knew her face had become red, yet her body still tingled. Her mind took command of her emotions, and she realized she was secretly happy that Jake had come by when he did. She gradually came back to herself, as she and Ryan followed Jake and Melissa back to their table. As they approached their table, they could see that the waiter was serving their desserts and soft drinks.

No sooner had they seated themselves and began to eat, the master of ceremonies stood and began to make introductions of those seated at the head table. It included the school's administrative staff and head coaches of each school sport, along with their spouses.

The spotlight was now focused on the athletes, their teams, and corresponding coaching staffs. Everyone was especially attentive as each team was introduced. The crowd stood in mass, accompanied by the applause of the attendees. Each coach singled out those on their teams who had earned specific awards and honors. Those recognized for these honors came forward to the awards table, which was situated in front of the head table. There the recipients received their awards from their coach.

Jesusha was nervous. She knew that she was going to be recognized for an award. It was no secret among the cheerleaders on the squad that she was the most valuable cheerleader. She was also the squad's captain, and the most highly-skilled tumbler on the team. She was a coach to many of them, helping them with their tumbling stunts and posing skills. She certainly was worthy of recognition, but the award was not given yet.

Although she had performed numerous times before crowds of people, this was different. Her performances were with the squad and not by herself. If she was called up to the awards stand, she kept thinking, "how will I walk up there, and what will I say: Everyone will be looking at me, and I'll be by myself." She quickly dismissed the thought. She knew she could handle it.

Just then she heard Ryan saying something. He was pulling on her arm. "Jerusha," Ryan said emphatically. "Get up. They are introducing the cheerleaders."

Jerusha looked around and saw all the cheerleaders who were scattered about the room standing by their tables. She quickly stood, realizing that her thought had so engulfed her thinking so that she was unaware of what was happening.

There was a thunderous applause echoing though out the room. All those in attendance knew the cheerleaders deserved this praise. They had performed marvelously and continuously throughout the school year, supporting the schools sport's teams. Their cheerleading team had three seasons: fall, winter, and spring. It was not like the seasonal sports.

The usual awards were announced and received. The awards were most improved, most inspirational, captain, and most valuable. In team sports the award recipients were also honored for offensive and defensive achievement. This was not the case for the cheerleaders.

The names of a few cheerleaders were read off while they were still standing. Her name was called, and she was embarrassed to be singled out.

"Way to go," Ryan exclaimed, while clapping his hands vigorously.

"You deserve it Jerusha," exclaimed Melissa, still smiling and now clapping. Jake, as in his usual manner, expressed his feelings of adulation for Jerusha by pounding the table with his two open massive hands, and let escape from his mouth a loud, very prolonged, shrill whistle.

All of this did not help Jerusha, who felt all the more embarrassed. She looked around at those at her table with a face displaying mixed emotions. One that said, in effect, 'I'm happy about this but please don't make it a show.' With that she turned and walked toward the awards table, where her coach and sponsor stood ready to honor her with the team captain and most valuable cheerleader award.

Jerusha returned to her seat quickly, smiling all the way. Once she was seated, she passed the awards around for all at the table to see.

"Neat," exclaimed Melissa.

"Congratulations," Ryan said gleefully, as he shared her joy. "Maybe I'll get an award," he said in a hopeful tone. "They always leave the football team for the last."

With that, they all sat back in their chairs to observe the remaining team awards. They were announced, along with their corresponding award recipients. The women's soccer team was next, and Melissa stood with them to much applause, although she did not receive any recognition. She was a good player, but had not yet met her potential. The coaches believed that this would be evident next year when she became a senior. After a good summer of playing club soccer, she would be prepared to fill the important position as one of the wings on the team in her senior year.

"You'll get yours next year," encouraged Jake, as he patted her on her shoulder.

"That's for sure," affirmed Ryan.

"Are you really going to play club soccer in the summer?" asked Jerusha curiously.

"I plan to. Probably will be all summer, if my folks will let me," responded Melissa.

"You know, Melissa, I've thought about attending an advanced cheerleading camp this summer…that is, like you, if my parents will approve of it, and then pay for it," Jerusha shared. She knew that she would probably have to work to help pay for such a camp. Most of them were far from home. She would have to fly, and she knew her folks would not allow her to drive to any of them. So, the cost would include more than just the camp fees.

Jerusha looked to see her date Ryan and his friend standing by, waving their arms slowly over their heads as though they were greeting every one of the guests in the ballroom. You would think they were getting ready for the kick-off in an important football game.

Jerusha almost laughed out loud. She now could see these guys as somewhat of a different type of athlete, almost like warriors preparing for a battle, while invoking the favor and supportive cheers of those sending them off to do combat.

It has been a long but a very good night, reflected Jerusha, as Ryan opened the car door for her at the close of the banquet. She settled back against the soft-leather covered seat, and continued to think on the highlights of the evening.

Jake received his award as the most valuable defensive player. He was extremely thrilled over this honor and kept saying, mostly to himself, 'man that's great, can't wait to show it to my Dad—I know he will be proud as can be.'

Ryan captured the most prestigious award. He was not only honored with the most valuable offensive player award, but the most valuable team player honor. Then to top it off, as a climax to the end of the evening ceremonies, the college scholarship awards were announced. Ryan and Jake received full football scholarships from the state university to play this coming fall.

Jerusha was happy for them. Full scholarships amounted to quite a bit of money. She was pleased also with herself. She received a scholarship from the same state university, but it was for tuition only. Still, this was unusually good, for seldom did cheerleaders get a scholarship before they tried out for the university teams. She felt a degree of inner satisfaction knowing this. She would have to prove herself. So, maybe, now, it would be to her advantage to attend the advanced cheerleading camp this summer.

Ryan had turned the radio on a station that played soft dreamy music this hour of the night. They had agreed to drive to the bluff which overlooked the lights of the town. Just for a look, at least, for a short time, before going home. On a clear night it was a beautiful sight. 'This would be a fitting end to a memorable evening, she thought.'

CHAPTER 15

Regrets

'I can't believe what happened last night,' thought Jerusha, as she recalled the events of the graduation banquet. She could not deny it. She had let her guard down, abandoned her conscience, set aside her moral standard, and had gone further in that pulsating intimate moment with Ryan than she ever imagined she could. She was no longer a virgin. That hurt her deep down inside, to the very core of her shattered heart. She could not blame Ryan, totally, although he had been persistently pursuing her seduction. She was aware of that, yet she should have been able to control the moment but she lacked the restraint.

She sought forgiveness from her God, the God of Abraham, Isaac, and Jacob. She knew that, although she had sinned, He had forgiven her. She knew that forgiveness, in part, was on the condition that never again would she succumb to the repetition of the conduct that transpired on that one evening of her life. She would never be able to erase from her mind. She continued to reflect upon the moment of her weakness, thinking that would change what had really occurred. She thought that she could alter the past by her meditation. Of course, she was fooling herself and she knew it.

"Jerusha, honey, are you awake?" yelled Rachael from the kitchen below. "Do you realize what time it is? Did you get in so late last night that you have to sleep so long?" she continued.

Jerusha rolled over in bed, looked at the red-numbered digital clock, and abruptly rolled over to the other side pulling the covers over her head. She did not want to face the world. She felt that everyone who saw her would know about her secret. Surely her guilt would be spread all over her face for anyone to see and know. Hopefully Ryan would honor her by keeping quiet. 'I need to talk to him soon,' she reminded herself.

"Jerusha," Rachael reiterated, "I'm not calling you again, you hear?"

Jerusha knew that her mom would probably send Ruth upstairs to pry her out of bed if she didn't answer. "Yes, Mom, I'm awake," she finally replied, "and I know what time it is," she acknowledged grumpily.

"Well, get yourself down here for breakfast. We are all waiting for you."

"Okay, Mom, I'll be right there." She got up out of bed quickly, which was usual for her. Normally she did not like to lie around in bed, but it was different today! As she slipped on her bathrobe and slippers on her way to the bathroom, the thought came crashing into her mind that God had forgiven her this sin, this transgression, and she too needed to forgive herself, and yes, even Ryan. She quickly rinsed her face, swished a little blue mouth wash around in her mouth, brushed back her hair, and bounced down the steps for breakfast announcing, "Here I come everybody, and have I got some good news to share with you!" (It was a happy talking voice.)

They were all sitting around that huge rectangular breakfast table. 'That's funny,' Jerusha thought, 'I never realized how large that table was and I've been eating breakfast here for years.'

Most of the breakfasts during the week rarely saw all the family sitting together. They were now situated with dad seated at his usual place at one end of the table, and mom at the other, while Benjamin sat on the side near the back porch door. Jerusha and Ruth occupied the side of the table opposite Benjamin.

Jerusha scooted in next to Ruth and smiled at everyone. Just as she was ready to tell the family of her good news, they all started clapping their hands and congratulating her for her accomplishments and the partial scholarship she was awarded. "How did you guys know about this?" she asked, beaming with pride from ear to ear.

"Ah, come on sis, it's all over the morning paper," Benjamin informed her. "But you're never up early enough on Saturday morning to read the news anyway. But it's great, sis, we are so proud of you!" he said somewhat apologetically for that verbal dig he laid on her. "Maybe," he thought aloud, "if I have some good football games the next few years I'll get a scholarship too, like you and Ryan did."

Everyone was quiet and looking toward Jacob. The food was on the table along with the drinks, but no one had touched a thing. "Well, dad," asked Rachael, "are you going to ask the blessing on the food and our day?"

"Sure, Honey," he replied, almost absent mindedly. He had been dwelling on how good God had been to Jerusha, and that now he might be able to afford to send her to college. "Well, let's pray," Jacob said, as he bowed his head over his plate. Everyone else followed suit. "Oh God, how grateful we are to You for life, for the day ahead of us. Help us to walk in Your Law and ways. Thank You for your gifts to Jerusha and bless this food I pray."

No sooner had he concluded his prayer but that little Ruth had already filled her plate with the morning victuals. "Ruth," Rachael addressed her, "you are supposed to wait until the end of the blessing before filling your plate and eating. It's not very lady-like!"

"I'm sorry, Mom," Ruth replied sheepishly, "but I was about to starve, and it looked like dad was never going to ask the blessing," she continued defensively.

Jerusha looked at her brother across the table and then to Ruth sitting beside her. She loved both of them more than she could ever express. Ruth was just a year away from becoming a teenager, and if she wasn't so much younger and shorter than Jerusha she could have posed as her twin sister. Both she and Jerusha were the very image of their beautiful mother.

Benjamin resembled more of his dad and had many of his facial features, but at the rate he was growing, year by year, it would not be long before he was taller and heavier than Jacob. Ever since he started playing football, in the ninth grade, his coaches had him on a yearly weight and flexibility training program. Now it was beginning to show. Those who knew the Goldenstein family always commented that they all looked alike.

Just as everyone was finishing their breakfast and were about ready to embark on their particular tasks for the day, Jacob reminded them of the family responsibility by announcing, "Don't forget our obligations to meeting at the synagogue later today. Don't be late. If you need a ride, be sure to be home in time enough to catch a ride," he added.

"Dad," exclaimed Jerusha as everyone was leaving the table. "I need to talk to you for a few minutes. It's important."

"Yes," he responded. "But not here. Ruth has to clean up, it's her turn, and we need to get out of her way," he explained. "Let's go in to the den," he offered, as he led the way through the kitchen, down the hall, and into an oversized, well furnished room, where they both sat down in large leather stuffed chairs opposite one another. "Well, what's so important that it cannot wait?" He thought he knew what was on his daughter's mind.

"Dad," she paused, as she took in an extra breath of air. "It's about college coming up soon. I need to talk to you about the money and all," she stammered.

Jacob was right. He pretty much knew what she wanted to talk about before she even addressed the topic. He knew it would be a financial stress on the family's budget, but with her scholarships he felt that it was a possibility. Also, if she was willing to continue her work this summer at the "Y" with the gymnastic team, as the assistant coach, she could earn enough money to offset some of the expenses involved in her freshman year at college.

"Dad, are you listening?" she continued.

"Yes, of course, Jerusha, we can supplement your scholarship with the needed monies to pay for your first year at school," he assured her.

A big smile spread across her face, accompanied by an audible sigh of relief. Just as she was about to thank Jacob for being such a great dad, he said, "You know Jerusha, your summer work at the "Y" will go a long way to help meet your college financial commitments."

Jerusha's smile instantly turned into a frown of disappointment. Jacob noticed it immediately. What did he say that disturbed her so? What could be the trouble that would bring such a change in her countenance?

"That's another thing I wanted to discuss with you Dad," she blurted out.

"Okay, what is it," he asked somewhat impatiently.

Just then, they heard a voice coming from the kitchen. "Ruth and I are finished here. How about you two?" Rachael called, as she stuck her head in the hall and looked toward the den. "Have you forgotten the time?" she continued. "Jacob, you have things to do and it is getting late for you too, Jerusha. They will expect you at the "Y" soon," she concluded with her usual reminders to them.

"Just a minute more. We've got a few things to finish here," replied Jacob. He got up from his chair and stood before her. He took one of her hands in his, and looked into her eyes with that fatherly look. He could see in her face that she was very concerned. He could almost detect a tear forming in the corner of her eye. He knew his beautiful daughter had a very sensitive nature. She was all business in her cheerleading and her work at the "Y", like she was a top sergeant in the way she handled her responsibilities in coaching and work.

"Dad, there's something else," she said, as she tightened her grip on his massive hand. "There's an advanced cheerleading school this summer that I'd like to attend and …" she paused.

Jacob knew his daughter well, perhaps more so than her mother. He knew that Jerusha did not take advantage of people. In fact, she was almost like a servant to many of her friends. She did not like to burden people, nor take advantage of her beauty to gain favor or special accommodations. So often the opposite was true—people took advantage of her sensitive personality and servant-like character. Jacob knew much about his daughter's personality and character was a reflection of her deep love and devotion to God.

Jerusha continued, "Dad, if I can attend this school, it's only ten days and it might qualify me, not only an advanced cheerleader, but perhaps I could become a student assistant coach which might pay me a stipend which could supplement some of my college costs.

"What's this student coach stuff?" Jacob exclaimed. "You're not even in college, and you already are an advanced cheerleader and a budding student coach, is that right?" he asked.

"Well Dad, I know it sounds too iffy, but it could happen. But without that certificate from the advanced cheerleading and coaching school..."

"Now the school or clinic, or whatever, is not only an advanced cheerleading session, but now it is a coaching session," he stated,

"Oh, Dad, look," she said, as she pulled a folded brochure from her jeans pocket and handed it to him.

Jacob took it and unfolded the brightly-attractive flyer. He leafed through it, viewing all the particulars of the school, noting the place, date, and cost of the many listed sessions.

"Was there something in particular you wanted me to see, Jerusha?" he inquired.

"Dad, look at those sessions that have the asterisks," she quickly replied, as she pointed to them as he held the flyer.

Jacob looked to where she was pointing noticing the gold stars at the highlighted sessions. These were special clinics on cheerleading coaching techniques, spotting, and safety management. He knew that, in a sense, she could well do what she thought might be possible, especially if she completed the school and earned that certificate. It could definitely be a profitable investment for all of them.

Jerusha could sense that her dad was mulling things over in his head. She had learned long ago to wait patiently and silently upon him to make a decision. She knew this was not the time for her to say anything.

Jacob looked up from the flyer. "Jerusha, dear, how about this for a deal?"

Jerusha perked up. She knew he was going to let her go, otherwise he would not have mentioned a deal. She was getting excited. "What's the deal, dad?"

"It's this," he responded. "I'll pay all your expenses for the school except the tuition fee," he paused. "I see it is five hundred dollars."

Jerusha winced. She didn't think it was a deal!

"It's going to cost plenty," Jacob continued, "with airfare and living expenses for some ten days. It will probably be at least four times the amount of the tuition fee," he surmised.

"Dad, it sounds like a good and reasonable deal, but can I earn enough money at the "Y" to pay that tuition fee?" But, she knew she could. She could work double shifts on their busy days, and it was still eight weeks before the school began—enough time to make the money (if she didn't spend it before that).

"You can do it Jerusha…get more hours and forgo our social and dating life for the next few months,,,you can do it!" he said assuredly.

Jerusha smiled, stood up from her chair, and hugged her dad while kissing him on the cheek. "Thanks, Dad, you're the greatest. I love you, and you don't have to worry about my social life, it's all gone. Most of my friends are off to summer school and internships. Ryan has to make up a class in math and then he is off to football camp with his buddy Jake. I won't see him, probably, until we enroll this fall at college. Our paths in the summer probably will not cross too often," she finished as she collapsed back into her chair.

"Well, then, that's that." Jacob concluded. "We'll get together and get all the details worked out. We've got time to do that."

Jerusha thought it would all work out just fine. She was bubbling over inside with pleasure like a pot of boiling water ready to bubble over its hot sides!

CHAPTER 16

College

'High school was never like this,' Jerusha thought, as she stood in line to register on her new college campus. Once that was done, she had to sign up for some of the classes she did not get pre-registering through the mail.

The line was moving rapidly, as she reflected upon the events of the past summer. The cheerleading school really did prove to be an advanced clinic. She was glad that she went. It was challenging at times, but she felt she got through it with flying colors.

Someone tapped her on the shoulder. She turned around to see who it was. "Ryan," she exclaimed excitedly, "it's really you. I haven't seen or heard from you for two months."

Ryan smiled, stepped forward and embraced her with his muscled 'T'-shirted arms, while lifting her up off of her feet with a bear like hug. "I tried to call you a couple of times while at football camp, but they work you to death," he said, as he returned Jerusha to the ground. "But your cheerleading camp switchboard operator told me you guys were not to be disturbed," he continued.

"Didn't you leave a message?" Jerusha asked.

"I sure did, even left my phone number."

"I never received any messages from you," she replied, somewhat puzzled. "I got my messages from my mom and dad, but none from you. Well what about that?" she queried, with a look of disbelief.

"I don't know, Jerusha, maybe it's a conspiracy," he paused with a sigh. "You know cheerleaders mess up the football players focus and all that. So maybe that's why. But I did call," he explained.

Jerusha had her doubts, but she was not going to pursue them here in line. It wasn't important now that they were both in school, she thought.

"Look, I've got to run. Practice starts in twenty minutes, and I've got to get suited up," he said hurriedly as he began to walk away.

"But…" Jerusha began to say something.

Ryan stopped and turned back to her. "See you tonight about seven at the ice cream bar tables in the athletic cafeteria," he shouted, turned, and ran off toward the football stadium.

Jerusha finally got through registration, and was even able to sign up for classes she could not get by mail. When the counselors saw that she was a scholarship cheerleader, they knew she had to have the afternoons free for practice. Besides, they did not want any run-ins with the coach, so they arranged her schedule to accommodate her afternoon practice sessions.

'That wasn't so bad,' she thought, as she headed back toward her dorm. Perhaps she will meet her roommate, Beth, who had already checked in, moved in, and was no where in sight when Jerusha moved into their dorm room.

Finally, arriving at the dorm, she entered the hall, dodged a half dozen girls moving into their rooms, and reached her room. The door was open. She looked up to see the room number mounted over the door—136. Yes that was the right room. Though the door was open, she didn't see anyone in the room.

"Hi there, you must be Jerusha," a cheerful voice emulated from the room. Beth walked out from behind the bed she was making toward Jerusha, who was standing in the doorway somewhat startled from the voice that suddenly came out of nowhere.

They both laughed realizing the situation. It was a good, but unexpected, way to initiate a new-found friendship right off, even though it was not planned.

Beth, who was starting her senior year at the university, extended her hand. Jerusha shook it while stating, "Yes, I'm Jerusha and it's good to know you."

"The same for me," replied Beth. "Come on in and let's get settled," she suggested.

"Our practice time is approaching, and this is our first practice with all the cheerleading team together. Hopefully everyone is checked in," she added.

Jerusha nodded approvingly, entered the room, located her bed, and sat down with a sigh of relief. "It's been hectic," exclaimed Jerusha. "Is it like this every school year?" she asked.

"No, it's better and easier after your freshman year, especially if you're an athlete or such," she assured her. "The school does just about all of it for you."

"That's great," stated Jerusha, "I'm glad the process is over! It's one I soon will not forget." They both paused, looked at each other for a few seconds, sizing up one another, and quietly realizing that their lives would now be entwined intimately as dorm roommates and cheerleading teammates.

"We better get ready," Beth warned as she broke the silence. "Our coach is emphatic about punctuality."

'The practice session went well,' Jerusha thought. She was showering after a very challenging workout. 'The coaches sure knew what they were doing,' she reflected. The whole team as a unit looked extremely good. She was especially pleased with Beth. She was undoubtedly the best gal on the team. Almost everyone looked up to her, and it was apparent that she commanded a great deal of respect.

Jerusha was excited. She knew, even after the first practice session, she would fit in very well, perhaps even become as good as Beth, in time.

"What are you doing in there, Jerusha?" spoke a hurried voice from the locker room. It was Beth. "I'm waiting for you and ready to go to dinner. Come on gal, move it," she urged, rather good naturedly.

"Okay, I'll be right there, please wait. I'll hurry," Jerusha pleaded. 'I don't know what happened,' she thought to herself. 'We both took showers together, and Beth was already dressed and ready to go.' Then she realized that she had been day dreaming in the shower. She must have washed every major body part at least three or four times. 'What a silly nut I am,' she determined.

They didn't go to the athlete's cafeteria. Beth told Jerusha she avoided it most of the time unless they were serving something really good, like pre-game meals.

"Why don't you like it?" Jerusha inquired. "Isn't the food pretty good?"

"It's not that," Beth paused with a smirk on her face. She shrugged her shoulders and said, "sometimes it turns out to be, like, a pick-up joint!" She concluded. "I'm sure you know about that," as she jerked her head sideways to get the hair out of her face.

"Not really, Beth, I haven't been to many places, like pick-up joints, that I know of, and I have only had a few dates."

Beth thought to herself that Jerusha had been somewhat sheltered. She seems to be a bit naïve. I'm wondering if she is Jewish, Orthodox Jewish. After all, her last name is Goldenstein. That must be Jewish. But, she liked Jerusha right off. She was sincere, pleasant, and extremely attractive, and after, the workout session ended, she concluded that Jerusha was a first-class gymnast and great cheerleader. She was excited about them rooming together. Already she felt like a big sister.

They arrived at the college cafeteria next to their dormitory complex, showed their ID's as they entered the large, crowded dinning hall. They proceeded to various food stations, selected a two-person table, and sat down to eat, all just in a few minutes or so.

"I like it here," admitted Beth.

"Besides, you can hang out with other than just athletes. Some students think all athletes are elite snobs. I hope by eating here I can dispel some of that."

"That sounds good to me," agreed Jerusha, "I have a boyfriend, or sort of. We dated a number of times, but not much in the summer. He has been off to football camp. We went to the same high school together. He's on scholarship, he and his friend, Jake. I guess they will both do fine," she surmised.

"We will be cheerleading at all the home football games and a few that are away. You will be able to see him a lot," Beth promised.

"I just don't know about our relationship though. I like him. He is a lot of fun and he has always been nice to me, but," she hesitated, "he is Catholic and I'm Jewish. My dad is very skeptical about our relationship." Jerusha smiled and blushed a bit, as if she was embarrassed about sharing some of her personal information with her new friend. "How about you, Beth. Do you have a boyfriend?"

"Well, now that you have asked," a big smile spread across her face displaying perfectly aligned sparkling white teeth.

Jerusha thought what an extremely attractive girl Beth is. No wonder she doesn't like to eat in the athlete's cafeteria. She probably would spend half her meal time warding off the guys!

"I do have a guy. We have been going together since our senior year in high school. His name is Morey."

"Is he here in school?" Jerusha asked.

"No, I wish he was. He's in the United States Coast Guard Academy in Connecticut."

"Oh, I see," acknowledged Jerusha.

"We planned to get married after graduating from our Christian high school back home," she uttered somewhat quietly, "but he received the offer to go to the Academy and it was too good to pass up. So he is there and I am here."

"Why didn't you get married anyway?" Jerusha asked anxiously.

"If you marry while in the Academy, they will expel you. They only take and keep single people until graduation," Beth explained. "We will just have to wait, even though I disagree with the policy."

They finished what little of the meal that they took. Evidently they were more tired than hungry, and as they were leaving the table to put their dirty dishes in the nearby racks, Beth stopped Jerusha by asking her, "By the way, what's your boyfriend's name?"

"It's Ryan Ortega. Oh my, what time is it?" Jerusha asked, as she looked at her watch, "I've got to meet him at the ice cream tables in the athletes cafeteria by seven. It's almost that now!"

"Here, let me take your tray and get going," volunteered Beth. "See you in the dorm. Don't forget curfew is at 11:00."

Jerusha barely heard her as she hurried out of the dinning hall to meet Ryan.

CHAPTER 17

Secrets

She was late. Even though she ran most of the way, she knew she would be late. Hopefully, she thought, he will be late too, with football practice and all, he'll be late. She was anxious and out of breath as she entered the ice cream parlor. She didn't notice how fancy the large room was decorated, nor the handsome white, wrought-iron chair and table sets arranged throughout the parlor.

She stopped and spotted Ryan on the far side of the parlor. She waved her hand and began walking toward him. As she walked, she noticed that another guy was seated with Ryan. She stopped momentarily to get a better look, and sure enough it was Jake Bronski. She hadn't seen him since the high school graduation banquet. She kept walking and as she got close to the table, both Ryan and Jake stood up. Jake got another chair from a nearby table, brought it over, and motioned with his hand for her to have a seat.

"Ryan, I'm sorry I'm late. I ran over here as you can probably tell," she exclaimed, as she wiped beads of sweat that had formed on her forehead.

"Oh, that's okay," Ryan said as they sat down together. "You remember Jake, don't you? continued Ryan.

"Sure do. Hey Jake, how are you anyway?" she responded.

"Just fine. Good to see you again, Jerusha. We have only been here a few minutes ourselves, so you are not really late. Let's just say that Ryan and I were early," Jake shared with a broad grin slowly spreading across his large face.

They all laughed. It was like old times in high school, where they all saw each other every day in classes, games and various outings.

"Ryan, when you stood up just now, I noticed that you looked bigger. Is that right?" she asked, seeking an answer confirmed by the curious expression on her face.

"You noticed that? I didn't think it showed," he proudly stated, as he stood to his feet, spun around one time, and sat down. "Look at Jake, he's even bigger. Didn't you notice that?" he inquired. "Come on, Jake, stand up and turn around so she can see that I'm telling the truth."

After a few silent seconds, Jake got up from the table, pushed his chair back, and slowly turned around.

Jerusha could see that Ryan was right. Jake was a lug. He was much bigger than the last time she had seen him, but he had always been bigger than Ryan. But not as much as right now! "He's gotten bigger than you Ryan," she offered as a matter of fact.

"You forget," he answered. "Jake's a linebacker. He needs to be bigger. I'm just a running back, and if I get too big it will slow me down."

"So?" mused Jerusha.

"I gained twenty pounds this summer, that's enough. But Jake gained thirty-five pounds," Ryan informed her.

"Enough of that," Jake declared sharply. "I've got to go. I have some phone calls to make," as he stood up from the table, smiled at Jerusha, waved at Ryan, and walked toward the door.

"I still can't get over how big you guys got and just in a few months," she said while looking at Ryan with a skeptical look.

"Jerusha," said Ryan.

"I'm listening," she returned.

"If I tell you something," he paused, moved his chair closer to hers, and leaned his face toward her. "Can you keep it confidential?" he asked.

"I don't know if I want to know Ryan." Jerusha was not sure she wanted to know something that Ryan called confidential. She did not like to keep secrets. She felt that when you did that, you became a party to other people's burdens or whatever. She had enough of her own secrets to bear.

She remained silent. Ryan could see that she was thinking about what he said, and he also remained silent so as to give her time to contemplate.

Jerusha was not thinking about Ryan but about herself. She had pushed an undesirable thought aside, pushed it into a corner of her mind, not willing to have dwelt upon it all these past months. Now it came rushing back into her conscious thought. She could not change it, nor even deny it. She had missed her period for three months since her unexpected intimacy with Ryan, who was now seated so close to her.

She had rationalized that the pressure and stress of her job at the "Y", her stressful activity at the cheerleading camp, and the anxiety of entering a new environment at college, all could easily cause her to miss her menstrual period. But, she had always been regular, and this was extremely unusual for her. However, she knew deep down inside that she might, probably, be pregnant. She had not shared her suspicion with anyone. At times she felt as if she would explode if she could not share this with a trusted friend! Perhaps this would be the time to share this with Ryan. After all, he was partly the cause of it. She pondered when was the right time and place to reveal this problem.

Jerusha looked full into Ryan's face and said, "Well, okay, what is it you want to tell me?"

"Sure you want to know?" he eagerly replied.

She hesitated, as a sly like smile spread across her still-sweaty face. "I tell you what, I've got something confidential," she whispered, as she lightly poked him on his shoulder. "Would you like to know? Can you keep it confidential?" she quizzed him.

By the look of curiosity on his face, Jerusha could see that she had motivated Ryan.

"Sure, I can keep a secret, especially if it is from you, Jerusha. You know you can trust me," he nodded, with an assuring smile, as he poked her on the shoulder.

"Let's trade secrets then," Jerusha concluded.

"Why not," he agreed, as he moved his chair even closer to her.

"You're first. After all you started it," she affirmed.

There was a pause in their conversation. It was as if each one was considering whether they really wanted to go through with the agreed exchange. Each one seemed to be thinking that this may not be such a good idea. Yet, it appeared that they both wanted to know each other's secret, and they were ready to accept the risk of knowing it, whatever it was.

"Okay, Jerusha," Ryan began, "you noticed a little while ago how much bigger Jake and I looked when you first saw us, and were probably thinking to yourself how that happened in such a short time," he asked.

Jerusha nodded her head affirmatively as Ryan continued. "Unknown to me, Jake had been taking steroids during the late spring of their senior year. He met some people who got him involved in using the drugs, convincing him he would be bigger, stronger, and faster by the time the college season rolled around. His chances of making the team as a freshman were greatly enhanced," Ryan continued to explain. "While we were at pre-season football training camp, Jake persuaded me to try steroids."

"Well, you are certainly bigger," Jerusha stated. "But are you better?" she asked with a stunted expression.

"Yes, yes to both questions, Jerusha," he stated. "But I began to question the practicality of it. It did help me, and I noticed no side effects, but Jake had been giving them to me at no charge for months." He stopped talking, drew in a deep breath, then another. "But Jake told me a few days ago that, from now on, I would have to pay him for the 'juice'." He paused again, his face became even more sober than before as he blurted out, "Jake is now a drug dealer, and he wants me to join him in selling drugs so that I can continue to pay for mine."

Jerusha was shocked. She wished she had never known this. It was pretty serious stuff, and she did not want to be implicated in any way. She never believed in taking any type of performance-enhancing drugs! She practiced sound and challenging programs of physical conditioning to achieve her success in cheerleading activities. To take drugs, to her, was a major form of cheating!

"Ryan, what are you going to do?" she asked.

"I'm not sure yet what I'm going to do."

"You've got to make a choice. You don't need that stuff," she declared. "You are good enough to play well without that, to be dependent on your own abilities and physical strengths!"

"I believe you're right. I'm leaning that way," he responded. "But I've got to go about this carefully, especially with Jake. He could be a problem." He fell silent for awhile, and under his breath uttered quietly, "I've got to think this through. In fact, I should never have told you," he confessed. "Jerusha, you never knew any of this, even if Jake asks you, okay, I don't want you involved," he pleaded.

"That's the best way to go, Ryan. The whole thing is buried with me," she added.

"Fine, let's not talk about it any more, ever," he emphasized.

"Consider it done," she concurred.

Again there was a silence between them as each collected their composure. The ice cream parlor continued to be a noisy place with students talking and laughing against the background of loud music from the speakers overhead.

Both of them were undisturbed by all the action swirling around them. They remained silent, cooped up within their own personal concerns.

Ryan looked at his watch, stood up from the table and said, "I need to go Jerusha. I've got a film meeting soon at the football conference room."

He looked rushed and anxious. Jerusha knew how important being on time was- especially for athletic meetings, but she had to share her secret with Ryan before he left! "Ryan, we haven't finished our deal yet," as she stood up facing him. "You need to hear my secret, please," she demanded.

Ryan stood there, shook his head, looked again at his watch then sat back down in his chair. "Well, hurry Jerusha. "I guess I can still spare some time."

Jerusha sat down and brushed some hair aside that had fallen in front of her eyes.

Ryan gazed at her. He thought to himself, how beautiful she is. I could really get serious about her, in spite of our religious differences. He continued looking at her face and waiting for her to say something, when he noticed tears beginning to wall up in her eyes. 'Wow, this must be some secret,' he imagined. "Jerusha, what is it?"

She seemed to gather herself, sat back against the chair, took hold of Ryan's hand, and said, "I'll try to make this as short and sweet as possible." Now the tears began to flow down her cheeks. She brushed them aside. "Ryan, since the night of the banquet, when we both lost control of ourselves," she paused, brushed away more tears. "Well, well…," she murmured, "I haven't had my period. It's been three months, and I'm really concerned."

"You don't think you are pregnant, do you?" he inquired.

Jerusha could see that concern was obviously displayed on his face. Was it for her, for him, or perhaps for both of them? She wondered. "I haven't had a test or anything," she replied. "But this is not normal for me."

"Look, Jerusha, this is serious. I don't have time to talk to you now with my meeting coming up, but I am very concerned," he assured her. "We can meet for lunch this Saturday, right here at one o'clock. That's three days away, okay?" He took her hand in his two hands, and held it firmly. Then, he stood up to go. "Please get a test before Saturday so we can talk about this, okay?"

Jerusha smiled, her eyes still moist. She stood up, facing Ryan and looked him in the eye. She then hugged him. "All right, I'll see you Saturday."

CHAPTER 18

Pregnant

'It was Saturday already,' thought Jerusha. How did it get here so suddenly? She found herself thinking about the past few days. What a whirlwind! Along with classes and cheerleading practice, she managed to squeeze in the purchase of a pregnancy test kit. It was positive! She expected that it would be so. How could it be anything else? She was not the type to disguise reality. After all, she admitted to herself, you don't miss that many periods and believe it was caused by some emotional disturbance you may have had. She knew herself better than that.

Still, she wanted to be sure that the test results were valid, so she made an appointment with a local pregnancy center for further testing. They affirmed it for her. She was definitely positive. How am I going to tell Ryan…and my parents! How was Ryan going to respond to the news? How were her parents going to respond to the news?.

"Jerusha, what are you doing?" Beth inquired. "You have been standing at the mirror, gazing at yourself for a long time. Are you in a trance?"

Startled by Beth, Jerusha popped her head around, looked at her and said, "you know I might have been. I've been thinking a lot lately."

"Yeah, I noticed you haven't seemed to be yourself these last few days. Are classes and the demands of cheerleading getting you down?" asked Beth.

"Maybe just trying to get settled in the daily routine has been a challenge," Jerusha responded. She reasoned that if Beth thought that was the reason for her recent behavior, it would be better than her knowing about the pregnancy.

"Well, I'll pray for you, okay? Just try to slow down your mind. Don't be thinking so much," Beth advised.

There was a pause in their conversation, as they both continued getting dressed for their individual activities. "Perhaps you'd like to go to church with me tomorrow," asked Beth. "I think you'd like it, and it may be helpful for you."

"I don't know. I'll think about it," responded Jerusha, with a non-committal tone in her voice. Jerusha knew that Beth was a Christian, and admired her for her belief and her lifestyle. Jerusha had observed her closely, and had come to the conclusion that her roommate was no phony. Beth knew that Jerusha was a Jewess; nevertheless, she kept inviting her to church. Underneath it bugged Jerusha, though she certainly was not going to share that with her.

"Wow, it is getting late," exclaimed Jerusha, as she glanced at the clock on the night stand next to her bed. "I've got to meet Ryan at noon for lunch. I don't want to be late," she added.

"Better get your reading in gear then," coached Beth. "I won't distract you anymore. See you tonight, sometime," she concluded.

This time it was Ryan who was late. 'Where is that guy?' Jerusha thought. 'It's been fifteen minutes and he's a no show!' Maybe this was a bad time. She thought they would meet in the lobby, and then sit down when they both arrived. But, that had not been the case. She noticed an empty table, and decided to claim it. Just as she was about to sit down, Ryan appeared in the entrance and spotted her. He waived to her and she waved back. She waited for him to make his way over to her.

"Been here long?" he asked with a smile. "Sorry, I'm late, Jerusha, you know how these Saturday mornings are."

"Yes, I know," she responded, as he stepped up to her, hugged her and kissed her on the neck just beneath her ear.

"You look great," Ryan continued. "Let's sit down. What's the news, Jerusha?"

Jerusha could see that he was upbeat in his demeanor, yet he seemed a bit anxious.

He's hoping for the best of news, but it is not going to be so. They sat down.

Ryan pulled his chair close to hers. "Do you want to get something to eat?" he asked. "Maybe a soda?"

Jerusha thought he might want to delay their conversations for awhile. "Are you in a hurry, Ryan?" she asked.

"No, not really, my afternoon is fairly free. No practice today, although I have a team meeting later."

"Well, then, let's get something to eat and drink. I haven't even eaten breakfast, and I'm fairly starved," she offered. She also thought it would be easier to break the news to Ryan over a meal.

At that, Ryan took her order, and went to the counter to put it in. He got his ticket number and returned to the table to wait for their food. He took Jerusha's hand in his, looked into her eyes, and saw a face without any makeup, yet, as beautiful as a spring flower. However, he could detect in her eyes an unsettled look, and realized this meeting is not going to bring good news!

Jerusha smiled, as she put her hand upon his hand. "This is not going to be easy Ryan," she said in a whisper.

"I figured as much," responded Ryan. "Well, what is it then?" he continued.

There was a silent pause between them as they continued to look at each other, not knowing what to expect from one another.

"Number eighteen," spoke a voice from the counter. "Eighteen, number eighteen," the voice repeated.

Ryan stood up, quickly walked to the counter, picked up the tray, paid for it, and returned to the table. He served the food off of the tray, set the tray aside, and sat down to eat with Jerusha.

Before Ryan could speak, Jerusha looked at him as a tear slipped down her cheek, "Ryan, it looks like I am going to be gaining some weight in the next few months, and without steroids." Tears continued to make their way down her cheeks.

Jerusha was definitely pregnant. Ryan felt a deep compassion for his friend. Yet, at the same time a feeling of commitment, though somewhat a reluctant one. 'What would happen now,' he thought. 'Football, marriage, school, fatherhood, and job?' All this ran together in disconnected thought patterns in his mind. He realized his world could drastically change! "So, you are pregnant?"

Jerusha put her soda down, picked up her purse on the chair next to her, and took out a tissue. She blew her nose and wiped her face.

Meanwhile, Ryan patiently waited for her answer. His heart seemed to be ready to pop out of his T-shirt. It was like waiting for a kick off, but a hundred times more intense!

"Yes, Ryan," she replied. Her eyes remained reddened and moist from crying. Her nose was running again, so she got another tissue from her purse. Before she could get it to her face, Ryan offered her his big, white hanky that he carried in his back pocket.

"Thank you, Ryan," as she wiped her eyes again. In a moment she gained her composure and told Ryan all of the events that took place in her life the past three days. "There is no doubt. I'm positive, Ryan," she stated, with a half-hearted smile brightening her face. "Both tests I've had have indicated this!" she added.

"Wow, does anybody know this?" asked Ryan.

"No, just you and me. I gave a false name to the clinic so they don't really know either," she explained.

"What about Beth, and your parents?"

"No, Ryan, just us, we are the only ones who know," she insisted.

"Well, what now?" Ryan asks.

"I don't know, it's all so confusing!" Jerusha commented.

Against his personal judgment, but wanting to appear as an honorable man, Ryan blurted out. "What about marriage?"

"Ryan, you don't know what you're saying. Thank you for being so considerate, but we are not in love. Maybe someday we could be," she paused, "besides my dad would kill me if I married anybody but a Jew, and you are a Catholic. We would be a fine pair!" she said emphatically.

Ryan knew she was right. They were not in love, 'but he could love her,' he thought. She certainly would make an adorable wife. She's a terrific gal, but there would be too many obstacles to overcome. Besides, what would happen to his schooling and football? Jerusha would also have to give up her schooling and cheerleading. He also knew that Jerusha would never convert to the Roman Catholic faith. His folks would not want him to marry a Jewess.

"Ryan, I could drop out of school and have the baby. Perhaps give it up for adoption, or keep the baby and move in with my family. Although I'm not sure how my family would respond to that," she exclaimed. "The other option is…" she hesitated, looked at Ryan with a apologetic, soft voice said, "is an abortion!"

There was a prevailing deadly silence between them, though the music was still throbbing through the speakers overhead. The students were still moving around them. For a moment they were in a quiet world of their own.

How could it come to this? This was serious. They both shared their personal thoughts. Yet, a decision must be made.

"Look, Jerusha," Ryan broke the silence. "Why not return to the agency and seek their advice, then go from there?"

CHAPTER 19

Decision

She was back again. She felt inside like the weather outside—dark, dreary, and drizzly. She hoped she was able to slip into the agency unseen. The terrible weather conditions had kept many people indoors who would otherwise be out and about. She thought, at least, that's a positive. Being seen in an agency like this could only cast suspicion on her. Yet, if she carried the baby to full term, everyone would know that she was pregnant, out of wedlock. What a blow to my parents and our friends at the synagogue! So many questions, so many looks and stares, so many explanations to offer—all these thoughts surged through her mind to the point that she wished it would all just go away. She knew it was just fanciful wishing. It would never go away.

Jerusha knew she would have to make a choice. It was not Ryan's decision. 'I am not about to be married for the sake of the baby.' In fact, they had both agreed that marriage was not the solution.

She had signed in at the reception desk, and taken a seat to wait for her name to be called. "Jerri Olden, Jerri Oreck," the receptionist announced. Jerusha heard the name, but at first it did not register. "Yes," she responded, as she arose from her chair and approached the counter.

"Hello, are you Jerri Olden?" she asked, as she looked at the sign-in sheet and then to Jerusha.

"That's me," replied Jerusha, thinking that this was the second time she had used the alias.

"Honey, just go in through that door on your left," the receptionist stated, as she pointed to the door. "Dr. Oreck will be with you in a few minutes for your counseling session. Have a seat." She returned the sign up sheet to the counter, sat down, and resumed her work without even so much as a second glance to Jerusha.

Jerusha entered into a large, well-furnished office, and sat in a cushioned chair opposite a massive desk. In fact, it was the only chair in the room beside the one behind the desk. There were a number of books occupying the book case behind the desk, and on one shelf she noticed a photograph of a man, woman, and two smiling children. They looked like twins about eight years old. That might be the doctor's family. No sooner had she thought that, when Dr. Oreck appeared from a door next to the desk.

"I'm Dr. Oreck. What can we do for you?"

When she left the office, she knew all the options that were available to her. They were mostly those she figured before the counseling session with Dr. Oreck. One thing did emerge, apart from assuring her that all was safe during and after the abortion procedure, the doctor advised that if she was to choose abortion, it would be better to have it performed as soon as possible. Also, there was a cost for the procedure, and she would have to sign certain papers, along with proof of her identity.

Jerusha immediately contacted Ryan. They agreed to meet in the student lounge, which was more like a huge, swank hotel lobby full of sofas, chairs, tables, and lamps. It was a convenient place to meet for sociable reasons, although some students staked out certain areas as their own for study purposes. They set the time for eight in the evening, for they knew that was the time when the lounge would be less populated with students. Later, they found a small sofa in the corner of the large hall, sat down, and began to talk.

"Well, how did you counseling session go?" asked Ryan.

Jerusha could see by the expression on his face, as he continually patted his knee, that he was more nervous about this than perhaps she was. "Ryan," she paused, bit her lower lip to stop its quivering. "It's not good news," she said quietly.

"What do you mean, it's not good news?" He responded, still patting his knee. "We knew there could not be good news, didn't we?" Jerusha swallowed hard. She felt that she was about to cry. She knew her eyes were misting, and now her nose was running. "Now, don't do that," requested Ryan, as he pulled out a huge handkerchief from his rear pocket and handed it to her.

"Thanks," she took the handkerchief, wiped her eyes, blew her nose, and handed it back to him.

"No," he said. "Just keep it for awhile," as he gently pushed her hand away. Ryan began to think about what Jerusha had said about it not being good news. It was puzzling. He pondered, 'what is not good news. You are either going to have a baby or not. Which is good news and which is bad news?' He concluded in his mind that it depended upon your perspective and circumstances.

"I'm going to have an abortion, Ryan," she blurted out, still wiping her eyes with his large handkerchief.

Ryan was shocked by her statement, even though he knew that they had both agreed that this was the only option!

Jerusha sighed and sat back on the sofa, as Ryan put his arm around her and pulled her to himself. He hugged her and continued gently to wipe her tears away as they rolled down her cheeks. They both sat there in a semi-hug position for a long time not saying a word, but both listening to the breathing of the other amidst a few intermittent sniffles from Jerusha.

She took the bus. She did not want to rent a taxi, or even get a ride to the clinic with a friend. She wanted this to be as secretive as possible. Perhaps because she was ashamed, or felt guilty, or was just confused—she wasn't sure, but she was aware of some disturbing feelings within her.

She got off the bus just a few blocks from the clinic, and proceeded to walk rapidly toward the building. She entered the waiting room, and signed in at the counter as Jerusha Goldenstein. No alias this time, as she had earlier arranged this appointment. This had to be legally correct. The receptionist smiled at Jerusha. "Honey, just sit there in one of the chairs. It will only be a few minutes," she assured her. "Oh, take this card number, number ten, and give it to the nurse when she calls your number," she added.

Jerusha took the card, number ten, she thought, 'I'm just a number!' No sooner had she sat down, looked at the card when the door opposite her opened. A nurse in a white uniform, pushing a metallic wheelchair, came out and announced, "number ten, number ten."

The Rubs all watched as Jerusha was led into the clinical room. She was assisted by a woman in white. As she lay on her back on the padded table, she was administered a substance that caused her lower extremities to be free of feeling, from the waist down.

After Jerusha lay there awhile, another person entered the room, dressed in white also, but he was a tall slender sized man. He would perform the procedure. Not much was said. The doctor went to the end of the table, and began to insert a long tube into her body. Then there was a sound like a suction of wind. The sound grew louder as the suction became more powerful. The end of the tube, before he inserted it into Jerusha, seemed to have a sharp end.

Although she could not see what was happening inside her womb, the razor sharp end of the inserted catheter was hacking One Fifty-Five into pieces, with the suction tearing him into small pieces completing his demise! The pieces of One Fifty-Five were forced into the tube, down into a bottle. The bottle was then thrown away!

Jeni placed her head into her hands. Robert was squirming in his seat through the entire showing, in disbelief of what he was watching. One Fifty-Five sat in his chair stoic-like, hardly moving, grimacing with every cut of the doctor's blade, as if he were experiencing it all over again. This was an abortion-the one they talked about between Jerusha and Ryan. It was really his killing. How could they! "That's enough!" he screamed. "I'm turning it off now."

"No!" shouted Robert. "Hold up, just pause it."

"Why?" questioned One Fifty Five.

"I've been thinking. Are we all involved in this story of Jerusha?" Robert continued. "Jeni and myself?"

"You've got a point there, Robert," Jeni chimed in, lifting her head that had been hidden in her hands.

"Look," asserted Robert. "Let me push my number in and see what happens."

One Fifty-Five was still acting frozen like, almost in a stupor, but he nevertheless saw the logic of Robert's request and pushed the pause button.

Instantly the screen paused. Robert quickly inserted his number 22,643,002. Immediately the screen brought Melisa and Jake into view. "So, I'm connected to them," surmised Robert.

"Pause it Robert and let's go back to One Fifty-Five," urged Jeni.

"Why," replied Robert.

"I think we are, like you said, all connected together, but our story starts with Jerusha,"

Jeni explained. "Let's go back to One Fifty-Five, push replay, then pause, and let me push my number in."

"Let's give it a try, if that's okay with you One Fifty-Five?" offered Robert.

"Sounds reasonable," replied One Fifty-Five.

With the entire button pushing completed, it was now Jeni's turn. She carefully and methodically pushed in 23,143,003.

As with Robert, the scene changed immediately. There on the screen appeared the figures of Beth and Morey.

It was true, as they had suspected, but now it was validated before their collective eyes. They were all part of Jerusha and her story.

It was obvious to all three of them. They would have to view the whole story in order to document their killings.

They all relaxed in their auditorium chairs, and pushed buttons that would take them back into Jerusha's story. Into all of their stories!

CHAPTER 20

More Secrets

It was over. Three days ago. What a relief! Jerusha was relaxed now, as she reflected about how nervous she was prior to the whole surgical scene. How apprehensive she was regarding the procedure. She doubted whether she could ever go ahead with it. But it was over, she thought again, now I can get on with my life! However, she did questioned herself! 'I gave up a life to go on with my life—was that a fair exchange?'

She was thankful that Ryan had obtained the money. She knew that Ryan did not have enough money, and she strongly suspected that somehow he had obtained it from his buddy Jake. 'If so,' she thought, 'I hope Ryan kept his promise about keeping this entire secret and didn't compromise me. Besides, now I am worried that Ryan may have obligated himself to Jake and his shabby dealings by helping me.'

She hurriedly dressed for cheerleading practice.

"You're not going to be late?" yelled Beth, as she was leaving the room.

"No way, I might even beat you there," responded Jerusha, as she saw the door close behind her roommate. She knew if she could leave in the next few minutes and run all the way to the gym, she could beat Beth since she usually walks to practice.

As she was running, she realized that she had more energy now than before. She felt better, almost as free as a bird, as she ran faster. She felt totally revived, and really alive.

The gym was in sight. She could see Beth on the walk just above her, and knew she would make it to the front steps before her. 'Some fun,' she thought laughingly. Then out of the blue, it dawned on her that she hadn't talked to Ryan, or told him about all that she had just been through. 'I know he's worried,' she thought.

"So, you did beat me," asserted Beth. "You must have run all the way."

"Well, I did," Jerusha admitted. "But I just felt like running," as a smile flashed across her face.

"Well, let's do it," urged Beth, as she took Jerusha's arm and they bounded up the stairs to the practice session.

Practice was finally over. Both Jerusha and Beth decided they would shower back in their dorm. Evidently they were both anxious to leave the gym today as they usually hung around the locker room after practice and mingled with the other girls.

They left quickly and promptly began their walk to the dorm.

"What's the hurry?" queried Jerusha.

"What's your hurry?" replied Beth.

They both smiled and broke out laughing.

"Well," Jerusha continued.

"Well, yourself," Beth responded.

"I asked first."

"Okay, you did," agreed Beth. "I'm expecting a call soon from Morey, at the Coast Guard Academy. He hardly has time for anything with his supervising of 'swab' year for the freshmen cadets. I've got to be in the room when he calls."

"Oh, so that's it," submitted Jerusha. "You've talked a lot about him, your high school sweetheart. Will I ever get to meet this dream boat of yours?"

"You just might. That's what he is calling about, a possible three-day pass to visit."

There was excitement in Beth's voice, Jerusha could tell. Even her face seemed to light up at just the mention of his name. 'She must really have it bad,' she thought, 'but that must be good, at least for her.'

"Now, it's your turn Jerusha. Got a secret or something?"

"Not really. I just need to contact Ryan. I've got something to share with him, nothing really special. Stuff from the home town and things like that," she explained. It wasn't an outright lie. After all, it all started with Ryan and her in their home town, she reasoned.

They reached the dorm room in what seemed like record time. Just as they entered through their door the phone rang.

"That's for you," yelled Jerusha.

Beth had already picked up the phone and began talking. Jerusha could tell right away that is was Morey from the Academy. Beth was all smiles.

She motioned to Beth that she was going to shower. Beth looked up from the phone, nodded her head, and waved.

In the shower Jerusha went over in her mind how she would share the news with Ryan.

It was good to see Ryan again. 'He has been so supportive through all of this,' she thought. Perhaps if they were both older, they might have been able to handle the situation differently. Then, thinking of their religious gaps, she concluded that a marriage would not work.

"Is it all over?" Ryan asked. However, from the look upon her face coupled with her pleasant, positive demeanor, he knew that the procedure had been successful. They decided they would not use the word "abortion." It was too explicit for them. "Procedure," they agreed, would be a better term.

"Yes, yes, thank the Lord Jehovah," replied Jerusha, as she stood up from the sofa where met earlier.

Ryan gave her a gentle hug, put his hand on the back of her head, and proceeded to kiss her forehead. They both sat down. It was apparent that they were relieved, and felt free from this long ordeal.

"I'm so very happy for you Jerusha," Ryan stated, in a consoling tone of voice.

"Thank you, Ryan, for your supportive attitude," she countered. "It was so helpful," she added, "not to mention the expense of the procedure."

Ryan smiled, squeezed her hand and said, "That's the least I could have done!"

"Still, thanks Ryan," she said emphatically, while smiling.

"Well, what's next?" asked Ryan.

"You've got football, and school and I've got cheerleading and school," answered Jerusha. "Then we both will see what life has for us."

"Yeah," nodded Ryan, "but football is over, as you know, the season has ended for us. We just missed playoffs by one win. We've had a good season." He paused, looked off into the far side of the hall in a trance-like state, then slowly murmured, almost to himself, "but there's next year."

Jerusha smiled, looked at Ryan, and said, "Yeah, there's always next year." Next year. The thought raced through her mind, 'what will that bring?' With that thought still on her mind, she stood up, turned to Ryan who was still seated, and said, "Look, Ryan. It's getting late, and I should be leaving. Thanks again for meeting with me. Let's stay in touch with each other, okay?"

"Sure enough," Ryan agreed. "Will do."

"Oh, Ryan, by the way," Jerusha hesitated, bit her lower lip, bent over towards Ryan, and then in a whispered voice asked, "is this procedure still our secret?"

Ryan's face looked a bit perplexed, as a few frowning wrinkles surfaced upon his broad forehead. He seemed somewhat disappointed that she would ask him that. 'I'm a man of my word. She must know that,' he thought. I guess she needs the reassurance. "Just you and I Jerusha, and it will always be that way unless you say otherwise," Ryan assured her.

Jerusha smiled, "I know, I should not have even asked you. I'm sorry," she stated apologetically. She turned to leave, looked back and said, "Ryan, don't forget to stay in touch."

Ryan stood up and caught Jerusha's hand before she got more than two paces away.

"Wait, Jerusha," he said somewhat urgently. "I need to tell you something important. Please, for just a few minutes. Let's sit down so I can share this with you," he pleaded.

"Ryan, can it not wait? It's getting late and I'm supposed to meet Beth soon!"

"Yes, it can wait," Ryan hesitated still holding her hand. "But it won't take long, besides I'm sure you would want to know this now. If I told you later, you would probably ask why I hadn't told you about this earlier."

Jerusha was convinced. She followed him back to the same sofa and sat down.

"Look Jerusha, this is somewhat confidential," Ryan began hurriedly to explain.

"Slow down, Ryan," Jerusha said, "I'm not that much in a hurry, besides I can't follow what you are saying."

Ryan settled down and began to speak slower. He started over again.

She could see he was somewhat nervous and a bit fidgety.

"Sorry, Jerusha," he replied. "I thought you should know this," he continued. "Jake is getting married soon, and it is supposed to be a secret."

Jerusha was surprised to hear that. She did not know anyone at the college that was dating Jake. It seems like he was all wrapped up in football with no time for dating, let alone marriage. "Wow, that's interesting!" she exclaimed. "Who is the bride to be?"

"You won't believe this," replied Ryan.

"I will if you tell me," she countered, a bit impatient with this conversation game of Ryan's.

"It's Melissa," answered Ryan. "Can you believe it?" he added.

"Why she's still in high school," stated Jerusha.

"Not anymore. She had to drop out—she's pregnant," he blurted out.

"You mean Jake's the father?" Jerusha asked. She was somewhat shocked at the disclosure Ryan had just made.

"Seems like they had been fairly intimate for some time before Jake graduated, and now she's close to giving birth. Jake promised they would get married after the baby was born," concluded Ryan.

"Wow, that's something," Jerusha responded. "I hope she is doing all right." She paused for just a moment, and thought that she was glad her situation was not the same. She wondered what kind of husband and father Jake would be. She just wasn't sure it would work between the two of them.

"Jerusha, remember this is confidential," reminded Ryan. "Especially as it has implicated me and, in a way, even you."

Jerusha was completely taken off guard by Ryan's statement. "How can I possibly be involved with Jake?" she asked, with an expression of unbelief.

"Look, Jerusha," Ryan said, putting his hand on her shoulder to reassure her. "It is confidential. I'll try to explain it to you."

Ryan began telling Jerusha how he had been implicated with steroid use and other things in his association with Jake. Since football season was over, Jake wanted Ryan to help him sell the stuff to other college athletes around the state. He explained how he had wanted to break this relationship with Jake. Jake, however, had brought up the fact that Ryan owed him 'mucho dineros'. Ryan had been involved in gambling, owed money to Jake, but had used the money he had saved to pay for Jerusha's procedure.

"Whoa, Ryan," interrupted Jerusha. "Does Jake know about my procedure?"

"No, of course not," Ryan answered somewhat perturbed. "That's our secret. Jake believes I used the money to pay off another wager I had lost."

"Okay, go on with the story," Jerusha said.

"Well," continued Ryan, as he proceeded to explain the rest of the story. It was evident that Jake was holding that debt over his head, and using it as a way to get Ryan involved in the steroid business.

Ryan continued to tell Jerusha of his conversation with Jake. He told Jake he did not want to be involved in his business, and that he would get the money he owed to him soon. He then offered Jake a deal that stated he would not tell anyone about Melissa and him, and also that he would keep quiet about Jake's business if Jake would forget him owing him money. Jake agreed to the deal.

"End of story," uttered Ryan. He had been talking for some time. Jerusha seemed to hang on his every word. 'Now,' Ryan thought, 'we both have more secrets to keep.'

"What a story," exclaimed Jerusha. "Now we have more secrets to keep—confidential like."

"Just what I was thinking," echoed Ryan.

"Now I know where the procedure money came from. Will Jake keep it a secret?" she asked.

"As long as we keep our end of the deal. But remember, Jake never knew about the procedure. He might have suspected it. But that is only a guess on my part," Ryan stated.

They both sat there thinking that things had turned out fine for both of them. The road ahead was clear and unobstructed. They could pursue life without any immediate obstructions.

Jerusha broke the silence. Looking at her watch she said, "Ryan, I've got to leave," as she stood up. "Beth's boyfriend is visiting, and I am supposed to meet them at the Hangar for dinner," she stated. "Look, why don't you come with me?"

"Not now Jerusha. I hardly know Beth and I don't need to meet some military guy!"

"Oh come on, it's not like it will kill you. Besides, you will get to know Beth better, and her boyfriend plays football for the Coast Guard Academy. You've got that much in common."

"Well, I don't know," he said grudgingly.

"Let's go," Jerusha prodded. "We can have dinner with them and secretly celebrate our new liberty."

Ryan reflected on Jerusha's last remark, and thought he had nothing better to do. He would like to talk football with another player. He smiled back at Jerusha, stood up from the sofa, grabbed her hand and said, "Well, let's go!"

Ryan and Jerusha arrived hand in hand as they entered into the newly-opened, campus-"elite" dining room. They immediately began looking for Beth and her visiting boyfriend. There was no telling where they would be seated. Beth had assured Jerusha that they would have a table of four, and that she and her friend would be on time.

It was the first time they had been to the new diner, so they did not know anything about the seating possibilities. The diner was decorated with a counter, and the type of old fashioned seats that usually accompanied the old time diner.

Ryan led the way, while Jerusha followed. They strode through the massive dining room looking for Beth. "Well, where are they?" asked Ryan, somewhat exasperated as he faced Jerusha. "Are you sure Beth said to meet here? They are no where in sight," he continued.

"That's what she said," replied Jerusha. "Beth usually does not make these kind of mistakes. They have got to be here somewhere, or they are late, which certainly is not like Beth."

Ryan and Jerusha stood there, in the midst of the dining room, looking at each other and wondering what they should do. Jerusha suddenly poked Ryan on the shoulder and exclaimed, "look!" as she pointed to an open door behind Ryan. Beth was standing there waving to them.

Immediately they gathered themselves, and approached Beth who was motioning them to come her way. "I'm sorry, you guys, it didn't dawn on me that you did not know there are two dining rooms in this diner. I didn't know myself until we got seated."

Beth paused, took a deep breath, while Ryan and Jerusha waited for her to finish her explanation and continued. "So, I figured you were looking for us in the wrong dining room since you did not appear to be showing up," she concluded.

"Well, is your Morey here?" questioned Jerusha.

"Sure is," Beth responded, with a huge smile on her face. "But, so is somebody else, or should I say so is another couple. You won't believe it!"

"Pardon us, would you please?" announced a strange voice. "You guys are blocking the door and we would like to get through, if you will."

Jerusha, Ryan, and Beth looked up from their conversation to see a party of people waiting for them to get out of the doorway so they could move through. How embarrassing.

"Oh my, we are sorry," announced Beth, as they moved away from the doorway. "I hope you were not there long," she ended.

"No, not long," a tall slender man, who was evidently not a student replied. "But you should find a better place to carry on your conversation," he admonished, as his party moved through the now unblocked doorway, and on to the second dining room.

"Let's see, what was I saying?" Beth continued, as the three of them regrouped inside the dining room. "Yes, you won't believe it, but Jake and his girlfriend, Melissa, are seated at our table. And Melissa is pregnant, as big as a balloon."

"I don't believe it. You're kidding?" responded Jerusha with a questioning look spreading across her face. "You don't even know Melissa, Beth."

"I know, you are right," replied Beth. "But I know Jake."

"But, but," Jerusha stammered.

Beth could see Jerusha wanted an explanation.

"As Morey and I were waiting for you guys, Jake and his pregnant girlfriend sauntered up to our table. Jake introduced Melissa as his soon future bride and mother-to-be of his child. Needless to say, I was somewhat taken aback," Beth continued to explain. "So, not wanting to be rude, I invited them to join us and you guys. Since they knew you folks would be joining us, they accepted our offer. We have been talking up a storm ever since waiting for you two to arrive. Now you know it all."

Ryan and Jerusha knew that the Jake and Melissa story was no longer a secret.

As they came close to the table, they both looked at each other and seemed to say by their glances to one another, that they would perhaps now find out the rest of the story.

As they approached the table, Ryan recognized Melissa immediately. Of course, Melissa was much larger than when he had last seen her. She still had that cute, young-for- her- age, look about her.

'The new person at the table, who stood up as they came near, must be Morey, the boyfriend of Beth,' Ryan thought. He remembered that Jerusha had said that Morey and Beth were high school sweethearts, and pretty devout Christians. Evidently their marriage plans were postponed because of Morey's stint at the Coast Guard Academy. It seemed a stupid rule, but it was binding.

So Beth came here to the university, while Morey went off to the Academy. Soon the four-year wait would be over for them. They planned to marry just after graduation this coming May. At least, that is what Jerusha had told Ryan. In fact, one of the reasons Morey was visiting Beth now, according to Jerusha, was to begin their wedding plans.

"I want you to meet Morey," Beth announced, as she made the introductions to Ryan and Jerusha.

"Jake and Melissa have already met Morey, and I've just met Melissa," she explained. "So we all know one another now." Beth paused, looked at everyone, and said, "well, let's sit down and order some food."

Ryan had conjured up in his mind an image of what Morey would look like, based upon some descriptive comments about him from Jerusha. She had seen a number of photos of Morey, and some of Morey with Beth. Ryan had never seen them, but made a mental image of Morey from the bits and pieces he gathered from Jerusha's comments. Morey looked like Ryan imagined. He was tall, 6'2", and weighed 209 pounds. He looked like a combination tight end and a wide receiver. He had a solid, well-built frame, accompanied with long arms and legs. His blondish hair, blue eyes, slender face, and firm jaw gave him an impressive appearance as a young man of 22 years. Ryan would have to admit that Morey was handsome. Beth and he made a very impressive couple.

No sooner had they all sat down at the table than the waiter appeared to take their orders. He was familiar guy who Ryan and Jerusha had seen on campus, but they did not know his name. Apparently he was another student, among many, who was working his way through college.

After everyone had given their orders, as if on cue, they all began to speak at the same time. It was a laughable moment. Each one at the table recognized this, and burst out laughing. The whole episode 'broke the ice,' and they settled down to the usual dinner-table chatter.

Jerusha was the first to speak as she looked across the table to Jake. "Jake, what are you doing here—and with Melissa? What a surprise."

Before Jake could respond, Beth chimed in with a long explanation. "Well, we were to meet you and Ryan in the big dinning room. We had already sat down at a table waiting for you two to show-up, and low and behold, who strolls by our table? It was Jake with Melissa. We invited them to join us, so we moved to this room for a larger table. That's why you had such a hard time finding us."

"Well, that explains it," responded Jerusha.

"Yeah, we had a time finding you," interrupted Ryan. "Although you found us," he concluded, as he looked at Jake with a questioned look on his face.

"Well, what is it, Ryan?" asked Jake, who often saw that look on his face, and recognized it immediately.

"Beth told me, just as we were coming to the table, that you and Melissa are getting married," replied Ryan. "Is that right?" he questioned.

"You got it right, buddy," responded Jake, as he drew Melissa close to him with his huge arm around her. Melissa sat there smiling and seemingly content as she nuzzled her head into Jake's shoulder.

"But, but," stammered Ryan.

"Excuse me, but we have your order," interrupted the waiter, along with another server as they began to serve the food to all at the table.

The table conversation stopped, as each person identified their order as it was placed before them. The conversation then continued. "Melissa, Jake, congratulations. That's great news!" Ryan stated, as he reached across the table and shook Jake's hand.

Jake shook his hand, almost knocking down the water glasses in front of them, and said, "Thanks, buddy that means a lot to me."

"Well, when will this happen?" asked Ryan.

Jake broke out with a big grin, paused for an instant, cleared his throat, and replied, "That's why Melissa and I are here. We wanted to know if you and Jerusha would be in our wedding."

"Funny thing," interrupted Beth. "That's why Morey came up here to visit me."

Silence fell among them as they all, one by one, turned their attention to Beth.

"What do you mean?" asked Jake.

"Well, I thought you might know. That is, I thought Jerusha might have shared that with you," she replied.

"And what is that?" retorted Jake.

"That Morey and I are getting married also. He is visiting me so that we can plan our wedding, and ask if both Jerusha and Ryan would agree to be a part of it," she concluded.

"That is funny," exclaimed Melissa. "Both Jerusha and Ryan are popular people," she continued. "Hopefully our wedding dates are not on the same day," she concluded.

"Hey," interrupted Ryan, "slowdown. This is good news for all of us."

"Look you guys, why can't we talk about this after dinner? The food is getting cold, and I don't know about you but I'm about to die of hunger," Beth blurted out.

"Sounds good to me," spoke up Ryan.

"Better yet, is everybody free tomorrow morning, say about 9 am? There is no school, and we could meet in the college study parlor and talk this through," offered Beth.

Everyone at the table looked at each other, as if to see if there was anyone who would not agree to her suggestion. It appeared that Beth's suggestion was one that suited everyone.

"Great," said Beth, "then it is a date tomorrow. Nine am in the parlor."

The group then began to eat their meal, as well as talk about college, sport teams, and such things that interested them.

CHAPTER 21

Special Decisions

The parlor was large, rectangular in size, with a high ceiling, and a floor, with stuffed chairs, sofas, tables, and lamps. As you entered into the parlor you got the impression that you had just stepped into a museum of stuffed furniture. About the only thing that brought the parlor into the college world of now, were the numerous paintings and photographs of college students, faculty and athletes adorning the walls.

Evidently the parlor was for comfort, informality and opportunity for quiet small-groups student sessions as if at home or in a library.

Beth and Jerusha were the first to show up. They were early, and had gone to the snack bar at one end of the parlor to purchase a pot of coffee, along with cups and condiments for their meeting with the others. They thought that it would be better to do this rather than wait for everyone to get their own. It would only prolong their meeting time.

They finally located an area that was close to the rest rooms, and began to arrange the furniture to accommodate all of them-all six of them.

Morey, who had spent the night in the visiting football dorm, arrived with Ryan a little after 9:00 am, and quickly located the girls as they were moving around the furniture.

"Need some help?" they yelled, almost in unison, as they saw the gals struggling to move a heavy, overstuffed sofa.

"Sure could," replied Beth, as she stood up with both hands on her hips.

"You came just in time," chimed in Jerusha. "Good morning," she added.

"Good morning to you," they both replied, as they stood before them. "Now where do you want this sofa?" asked Ryan, in a manly tone.

With that, Beth and Jerusha told them how their little party of chairs and sofas should be arranged for their meeting. No sooner had they finished arranging the furniture, than in walked Jake and Melissa hand-in-hand.

"Hey, guys, you are just in time," blurted Ryan. "Come over, have a seat, and have some coffee."

"Thanks, we will just do that," replied Jake, as he and Melissa took a place, side by side, on the sofa. "Sorry we are a little late. I had to go by the visitor's dormitory to pick up Melissa and she was not quite ready."

"That's right," Melissa confirmed. "It's my fault we are late."

"No big deal. Let's get started on these weddings, okay?" Beth stated.

Jake explained to them that he and Melissa wanted to marry before the baby was due, which was real soon, and they wanted a private ceremony with just themselves and some witnesses. He went on to reveal that Melissa's family was not very happy with the situation, and had wanted them to wed after the baby's birth. They also did not think her parents or his parents would attend the wedding, for they and their church were not very happy about the situation.

"I'm sorry to hear that," said Jerusha, as Jake paused to clear his throat while taking a drink of coffee. "Well, where and when is this going to happen Jake? Do you have any plans?" she continued.

"Yes, we have plans, and we would like you and Ryan to stand up for us," he replied. He and Melissa had thought their plans through. "It will be three weeks from today in the university chapel, at 10 am." He paused, took another drink of coffee. "We already have it reserved, but, as of yet, do not have the school chaplain to conduct the ceremony. He thinks he might have a conflict in dates. But somehow we can work that out. In the meantime, we already have the paper work necessary for the marriage."

"Are you with us, and are you free at that time Ryan and Jerusha?" Melissa implored. "We don't know who else to which we can turn."

Jerusha knew in her heart that she could not disappoint them. She was thankful she was not pregnant and not getting married. This is the least she could do for them. She looked at Ryan to see if there was any hint on his face as to what he was thinking. Ryan was looking at her also and it seemed, though nothing was said, she could see in his eyes that he too was not going to let down his friends.

"Can we do it Jerusha?" Ryan quietly said.

"Without a doubt," replied Jerusha.

"Then you can count us in," responded Ryan, as he turned to Jake and Melissa and extended his hand to seal the deal. As he did so, he noticed the tears of joyous relief flowing down Melissa's cheeks.

"Oh, thank you guys!" exclaimed Melissa, wiping away a tear from each eye.

"You're the greatest. We just knew we could count on you two," echoed Jake, as he vigorously pumped Ryan's hand.

Meanwhile, Beth and Morey sat there, quietly drinking their coffee, and taking in the whole scene.

"Look, now that that is settled, what do Ryan and I do?" asked Jerusha.

Jake answered immediately, "Just show up about 30 minutes before 10:00 AM three Saturdays from now at the chapel."

"What about dress?" asked Jerusha.

"Just informal, in a little more than school dress," replied Melissa. "I am not wearing anything too fancy," she continued. "A pretty pink dress and heels. Jake thinks I look good in pink." She blushed as she smiled.

All was quiet for a spell, as they returned to drinking their coffee. Then suddenly, it seemed to dawn on those embroiled in the wedding arrangements of Melissa and Jake that they had completely ignored Beth and Morey who had silently sat through all of their discussions.

"Beth, Morey. Man, we forgot all about you," declared Jerusha, apologetically, as if speaking for the others.

"No problem," stated Beth.

"Yes, but you two are getting married also," exclaimed Jerusha. "How can we help you?" she added.

Beth smiled, sat upright in her chair, and reached over to take Morey's hand. "We are getting married right after graduation. It is here in the ROTC Naval Chapel on campus on the Saturday after graduation. It will be somewhat of a military-type wedding, but not completely military." She paused, looked around, and saw that she had their attention, so she continued. "We, that is Morey and I, would like you, Jerusha and Ryan, to be part of our wedding ceremony also. That is, if you will be willing to do this?"

"I'm not going anywhere for a few days after graduation. You can count on me, and I think Ryan can do it too." Jerusha stood up while talking, and did a high cheerleader kick while clapping her hands.

"Well, thanks for speaking for me Jerusha," responded Ryan, a bit sarcastically. "Just happens that I've got to be around for some post-graduation football stuff, and more than likely I'll be available. And besides," he surmised while looking at Morey. "We football buddies need to stick together."

"Cool, that's great. But there will be a rehearsal the day before the wedding when our pastor will come up to conduct the wedding. Will that be a problem?" Beth asked.

"Probably not," replied Jerusha.

"Okay by me," agreed Ryan.

"Great, I'll keep you informed on all the goings. Maybe we can meet some time earlier, to get all things squared away," assured Beth.

"Hey, Beth," interrupted Jake. "Could your pastor wed Melissa and me?"

Beth thought for just a moment and said, "I'm not sure about that. Morey would know more about that possibility than me. Ask him."

"Well, Morey," asked Jake. "What's your take?"

Morey heard Jake's question, but he was slow to answer. In fact, he wasn't quite sure what to say. He was not sure if either Melissa or Jake were Christians, not just church-going people, but truly spiritually-born Christians with their faith in Jesus, not just in a denominational church.

"Well Morey," Jake urged, "what about it?"

Morey looked at Jake and could see some anxiety expressed in his face. 'How can I answer his question candidly and kindly and truthfully?' he thought. Finally Morey said, slowly but clearly, "As far as I know, the pastor in our church really serviced mostly only church members and relatives of church members."

"Oh," responded Jake. "But what about Melissa and me, could he do it?"

"I'm not sure. I really can't speak for him," responded Morey. "But one thing I know," Morey hesitated. "Well, I think I know."

Jake interrupted saying, "What's that?"

"Well, he gladly marries Christians," Morey replied softly.

Jake was taken back by that statement, and Melissa seemed to snuggle more into Jake's arm as if trying to hide-hide from perhaps her pregnancy out of wedlock. 'Why,' she thought, 'would a pastor marry Jake and me knowing our circumstances?'

"Melissa and I both belong to our own churches, and have been members ever since we were confirmed," retorted Jake. "Isn't that right Melissa?" he continued, as he looked into her face.

Melissa sat up straight with a concerned look and said, "Yes, that's absolutely right, Morey."

"That's all well and good Melissa," interjected Beth, "but church membership doesn't make you or me a Christian."

"How do you know, Beth?" demanded Jake. "And for that matter, what is a Christian anyway?" he questioned, in a forceful voice.

"O, look Jake," stammered Beth. "I did not mean any harm. I'm sorry if I offended you and Melissa, but I just wanted you to know the truth, if you didn't know it already," she concluded apologetically.

"Truth-truth about what?" questioned Jake.

"Excuse me Jake," Morey butted into the conversation with a wave of his hand. "It's like getting the plays right in football, in a way, that is, in order to win," he continued. "Well, to get to the point. A Christian, according to the Bible, is one who has acknowledged Jesus Christ as Lord and Savior of his life, believes Jesus died for all of his sins, that He is resurrected and alive, and has called upon Him to save him," expounded Morey. "It's as simple as that! When I was four years old, I decided to receive Jesus Christ as my Savior and Lord, and I sure was not a member of any church at that time. So believing in and receiving Jesus into your life is what makes you a Christian," he surmised.

Quietness fell on all seated around their table. No one talked. It seemed that what Morey had just shared was foremost on their minds.

Beth and Morey were silent also, and both were praying quietly for these friends salvation, as they had done so many times in days past.

Jerusha broke the silence with a whispered question. "Where do you find this truth in the Bible?" as she looked to Morey for an answer.

Morey smiled affectionately, looked to Jerusha and said, "God's truth is all over the Bible, but the truth that really concerns us living in this day and age comes mainly from the New Testament and Paul's Letters to people of his day and today.

Jerusha winced. She could feel something in the pit of her stomach, like something dreadful was going to occur. "You mean the truth is in the New Testament? Isn't the Old Testament truth good enough?" she questioned. She knew that the Old Testament was the Bible for the Orthodox Jew. The New Testament was almost a forbidden Book, she had never read it, nor was she familiar with it. She was reluctant to pursue it any further, after all she was a good Jew. Except, she remembered her actions with the baby she had aborted, and somehow felt her actions were not considered good. In spite of her doubts, she decided to listen to what Morey was saying.

Morey nodded and gave her a reassuring smile. "Well, Jerusha, as you know, the Bible for thousands of years has historically and traditionally been considered comprised of both the Old and New Testament.

"We know that," Jake interrupted rather impatiently. "But what is a Christian from the Bible, like Jerusha asked?"

"Well, okay," conceded Morey. With that he pulled from his right back pocket a red-covered, worn New Testament, opened it and said, "Jake, Melissa, Ryan, and Jerusha, as well as myself and Beth." He paused as he thumbed through the pages of the Book he held in his hands, stopped in a certain place, looked up and continued. "We are all sinners in God's sight and cannot go to Heaven in our sinful state!"

It was as if a bomb of silence had exploded among them. You could have heard a pin drop.

Morey quickly read to them from Romans 3:23. "For all have sinned and come short of the glory of God." Then he flipped a few pages over to Romans 6:23 and quickly added, "For the wages of sin is death, but the gift of God is eternal life through Jesus Christ our Lord."

Silence still lingered among the group. The Holy Spirit appeared to be so evident now, as He had captured their attention almost immediately. It was as if they anxiously were waiting for the next set of Scriptures for Morey to read.

Morey continued, "God knows we were lost and on our way to Hell. So in His love and sovereignty, He sent His Son Jesus to Earth to be our Savior. He came as a little baby. The writer of the Gospel of John said," continued Morey, "for God so loved the world that He gave His only begotten Son, that whosoever believeth in Him should not perish but have everlasting life."

He continued, "Certainly you all have heard of this verse. You have even seen this at some football games where some guy in the stands would hold up a big sign that was printed with John 3:16. This was, in a sense, a birth announcement of Jesus coming as a babe into the world of men. He was to live and then die on the cross, the God-man, for the payment of our sins against God and man. Then, those who believed in Him would receive forgiveness of their sins forever, and be given the gift of eternal life through Jesus," he concluded.

Morey drew in a breath of air, looked around, and could see that the Word was taking affect. "Look," he said, "Jesus died for all men's sins, but He did not stay dead, as you might know. On the third day He arose from the tomb, and now lives in His resurrected glorified body in Heaven with the Father. It's right here," he continued, as he turned more pages of his red-worn New Testament. "It's Paul again writing in Corinthians-listen. 'Moreover, brethren, I declare unto you the Gospel which I preached unto you which also ye have received, and wherein ye stand: by which also ye are saved, if ye keep in memory what I preached unto you, unless you have believed in vain. For I delivered unto you first of all that which I also received, how that Christ died for our sins according to the Scriptures; and that He was buried and that He rose again the third day according to the Scriptures.' Now, that's right from I Corinthians 15:1-4," finished Morey.

"I think we know that," said Ryan.

"Yeah, for sure," chimed in Jake. "We celebrate mass in our church. We know Christ was crucified," he insisted.

Melissa nodded her head in approval.

Jerusha, though, was somewhat perplexed. This was somewhat new to her, and she was taken aback in her mind about what she had just heard.

"Okay you guys," responded Morey. "Just think this through. Was it a church that hung and died on the cross for your sins and mine? You know the answer. It was Jesus Christ and He alone that died and rose again. No church ever died for you or rose from the grave."

"So that's true for sure?" stated Ryan. "It certainly makes sense, but what makes you a Christian? Or, as Jake said, what is a Christian anyway?"

"Fair question, Ryan," responded Morey. "It's what you do with what you know. Paul clearly says in this great Roman letter of his, 'if you shall confess with thy mouth the Lord Jesus and shall believe in your heart that God hath raised Him from the dead, you shall be saved. For with the heart man believeth unto righteousness; and with the mouth confession is made unto salvation. For the Scripture says, whosoever believeth on Him shall not be ashamed. For there is no difference between the Jew and the Greek: for the same Lord over all is rich unto all that call upon Him. For whosoever shall call upon the name of the Lord shall be saved.'"

A lightning bolt hit Jerusha right in the heart-no difference between the Jew and the Greek. That was a revelation! Jesus is Lord of both, and is rich to all them that call upon Him. 'What a marvelous truth,' she thought. 'I never knew this, or at least understood it. So that's how one becomes a Christian. 'How easy and so extraordinary,' she thought as she burst out laughing and crying at the same time, while clapping her hands repeatedly!

Tears began to well up in Beth's eyes as she moved over to Jerusha and hugged her. They both sat there looking at one another, holding hands, smiling and laughing together. What an astounding moment! The Spirit of the ever present God was there in their midst and working!

Melissa, Jake, and Ryan were dumbfounded as they sat in their seats observing Jerusha and Beth.

Morey cleared his throat and said, "That's how you become a Christian. That is, if you believe and do what I just read to you from Romans 10: 9-13. Simply acknowledge that Jesus is Savior and Lord in your mind, and believe in your heart that God raised Him from the dead, and call upon Jesus to save you. Instantly you will be a child of God, and one of His Christian saints. That's it! In a Bible nutshell so to speak."

Again, there was silence among them. All eyes were upon Jerusha and Beth. They were transfixed on the two young ladies who were holding hands while sobbing and laughing together. It was as if they wanted to cement that scene permanently into their minds as they continued to stare at them.

After awhile, Ryan got up and moved over to Jerusha, sat on the arm of her chair, put his arm around her shoulders, and gave her a kiss on her forehead. He then whispered in her ear, "Jerusha, that's great. I'm so happy for you."

Meanwhile Melissa and Jake got up, walked over to Morey, and Jake extended his hand and said, "Morey, thanks for telling us those things. But my church has confirmed me, so I'm okay, and it's the same with Melissa."

Morey shook Jake's hand, turned to Melissa, smiled, took out a couple of Christian tracts and said, "Here, you guys, take these home, if you will, and read them. It's what I just shared with you. There are also a few more things about becoming, and being a Christian," he concluded.

Both Melissa and Jake took them as they began to leave, but stopped long enough to say goodbye to those huddled around Jerusha. "We will stay in touch with you about the wedding, Jerusha. And we will see you soon Beth," expressed Jake, as he waved his hand in a goodbye gesture and left the room with Melissa.

Morey could see that it might be best to leave Jerusha and Beth alone for awhile, so he suggested to Ryan that they wait for the girls outside.

There was no verbal response from either Jerusha or Beth, but they both looked up with tearful eyes and nodded their heads.

With that Ryan and Morey left the room, and on the way out, Morey gave Ryan one of the tracts he had just offered to Melissa and Jake. "Those verses in Romans, which I shared with you, are in this little booklet, Ryan. Hopefully you will take some time to read it."

"Thanks," responded Ryan as he took it and slipped it into his back pocket as they exited the room.

CHAPTER 22

Another Decision

"Morey, are you awake," whispered Ryan, as he slipped his head into the room, which was used for visiting teams while visiting campus. Morey had been staying there while visiting campus these past few days. "I can't sleep, if you don't mind, can we talk?"

Morey was asleep, but he didn't mind being awakened. He had gotten used to it at the Academy. No night was sacred there!

Ryan, seeing that Morey was aroused, kept talking. "Ever since we took the gals back to their dorm, I have been thinking about those things you shared with us. I just need to talk," he said emphatically.

"Come on in, but don't turn on any light yet. Leave the door open," responded Morey as he got up, put on his robe, and turned on the bathroom light just to lighten the room up a bit. "Can't stand a lot of light first thing," explained Morey, as he motioned Ryan to take a chair next to his bed. He sat back on the bed.

They both remained silent for a moment while adjusting their vision to the dim light. It was a bit awkward. Neither of them knew each other at all. They had just recently met. The only connections in their lives were football and Beth.

Ryan adjusted himself on the chair moving it closer to Morey's bed. It was 1:30 am. "I didn't realize it was this late," admitted Ryan. "I'm sorry."

"No problem, Ryan. You get used to this at the Academy," he paused, and with a reluctant grin said, "they wake you up at all times of the night or morning. So what is it?" he questioned.

"Well, what you said about a church never hanging on the cross for my salvation, only Jesus did. That really struck me. The more I thought about it, I knew that it was true. So many people, like me, believe the church is our door to salvation and Heaven. It's Jesus and Him only!"

"Boy, Ryan, the Lord must have revealed that to you!" marveled Morey. "Have you read that little booklet I gave you?"

"No, not really, just briefed through it. I've got it with me though."

"Well, let's go through it," suggested Morey.

They both huddled around the tract as Morey led Ryan through it page by page.

God is the only God, a loving God, but a just God. He must punish sin and the sinner by not allowing him into His Heaven, but in His love and grace, He sent His Son to be the propitiator for man's sins. By believing this and calling upon the risen Lord to save him, the sinner is set free and bound for Heaven by the grace of God simply by exercising one's faith.

Morey covered all the bases. Ryan was completely attentive, following every word of every page. Finally they came to the page where it challenged the reader to call upon the Lord for salvation.

Morey looked up from the booklet and Ryan's eyes were fastened on him. He could see the Spirit was working in him! "Ryan, are you ready to call upon the Name of the Lord to save you."

Without hesitation Ryan said "Right on! What do I do?"

"Do just what it tells you to do," urged Morey.

"From what I understand, the Lord died for my sins and God raised Him the third day as proof of this. Through Jesus I can have eternal life if I believe what the Bible says," Ryan stated.

"That's right, but you need to call upon the Lord, in faith, to save you," challenged Morey. "If you believe what I am saying and if it's what you want to say yourself, then you can pray along with me," he suggested. "Does that sound okay?"

"Sure, why not?" answered Ryan.

Both of them were seated, and Ryan looked to Morey, who bowed his head and began praying. Ryan immediately followed. "Dear Jesus, I acknowledge you as my Lord, and believe you have risen from the dead after paying for my sins on the cross." Ryan repeated the prayer.

"You have given me eternal life, and I call upon your Name, Lord, to save me. Thank you Lord, Amen." Ryan repeated the prayer again.

They both looked up and Morey could see traces of tears trickling down Ryan's cheeks accompanied by a smile that expressed peace and joy.

"I'm saved. Is that true?" asked Ryan.

"You are. Did you not do what the Lord asked you to do?" asked Morey.

"I sure did," responded Ryan.

"Then, it's a done deal. God does not lie. He keeps His word," assured Morey. "You are now a Christian-a child of God's eternal spiritual family!"

"So, what's to do now?" queried Ryan, with a puzzled expression, as he wiped away the remaining tears on his cheeks.

"It's a new life, a new way of life, a new way of living," Morey paused, got up, and went to the nearby desk where his Bible lay. He picked it up and said, "This is your play book. You need to read it and live according to it, especially in the writings of Paul, who is God's chosen minister for the church today. You should start reading it tomorrow. I'd recommend you start in the book of Romans," he concluded, smiling from ear to ear. Morey was rejoicing over Ryan's decision to call upon the Lord. It was written all over his beaming face.

"Congratulations, Ryan. You and I are now spiritual brothers, and I believe that the same thing happened yesterday to Jerusha. She is now our spiritual sister. That should be good news to you!" Morey exclaimed.

This was different, thought Jerusha. Ryan was sharing the same thoughts. Both of them had never been in a Protestant church before, except for weddings and funerals. Never for a church service! They both felt out of place, but Beth assured them it was alright to be a little nervous. "Just take some time to settle in, look around, and you will be fine," she assured them.

Students and young professionals attended the Sunday school class. There were about twenty in all, plus the married, middle-aged couple that was leading the class.

"What are we doing here?" whispered Jerusha into Ryan's ear, as they shared adjoining chairs.

"You know why," responded Ryan. "It was Beth's idea, remember?" he quietly continued.

"Yes, that's right. She gave us a good reason, I believe, when she told us you are now Christians. So it is time to start knowing and growing in the Word of God," remarked Jerusha.

Beth's short statement had taken hold of both Jerusha and Ryan. They knew she was right. You can't grow in Christ unless you grow in His Word. Somehow they knew this to be true, even though individually they had never studied the Bible. In fact, the New Testament was a sealed book to Jerusha, and Ryan's understanding of the Bible was given to him by his church which left much to be desired. So this little Sunday school class was a new experience for both of them. Little did they know then that it would become a great and important part of their spiritual lives.

The couple leading the class introduced themselves, and mentioned that both had graduated from college years ago. She had become a football wife because Dave (her husband) played in the Canadian Football League where Dave found the Lord through some guys from Athletes in Action, an organization known as Campus

Crusade for Christ. The woman then asked others to introduce themselves just before the Bible study began.

Both Jerusha and Ryan were a little hesitant, but Beth came to the rescue by introducing them as her friends. Then she added they are new Christians, which drew the applause of those in attendance as well as a few 'amen's.'

After everyone had settled into their chairs, Dave, who Ryan thought 'must have been a middle linebacker because he was so big,' began by asking them to turn in their Bibles to Acts, chapter eight and nine.

Morey, sitting on the other side of Ryan, nudged him. "Dave was an All-Pro in the CFL, and one of the better players to come out of that league," he quietly stated.

Dave read the chapters aloud, and explained them in light of Paul's experience. An interesting aspect of his presentation was as he noted: Paul (the Apostle) met the Lord on the Damascus Road, and was converted to Him and His will. Paul, who was a Jew and followed the Mosaic Covenant, was also a Roman citizen of an empire that was composed of pagan Gentiles. Interestingly enough he, Paul, represented both peoples for which Jesus died.

Beth glanced over to where Jerusha and Ryan were sitting with the Bibles she had given them. They opened them to Acts, and they both seemed enthralled. She smiled inwardly and thanked the Lord.

CHAPTER 23

Do Right

"Jerusha, you need to pray about doing this," counseled Beth, with a voice most sympathetic but yet challenging. "Ryan needs to do this also," she added emphatically.

Morey had gone back to the Academy right after lunch Sunday afternoon, but not before Jerusha and Ryan both promised that they would read their Bibles daily, starting in the book of Romans. They would also attend Beth's church, as well as the weekly Bible study on Wednesday evenings.

"No, I can't," replied Jerusha sobbing.

"You mean you won't pray about this?" questioned Beth.

"Oh, no, not that. I'll pray, but I can't do what you suggested," as tears ran down her cheeks.

Jerusha, after her startling, but genuine, conversion to the Lord Jesus, confided in Beth about her intimacy with Ryan, and the resulting abortion of their child. In such a short time, the two girls had become like sisters, with Beth as the older. Jerusha trusted Beth and was eager for her friendship and her counsel. "They all will disown me, even my brother, Benjamin, and Ruth, my sister," she explained, as she dried her eyes from the tissue nearby. "I've got three strikes against me before I ever get to see them, yet alone talk to them. They will never forgive me!"

"They love you, don't they?"

"Yes, but I don't think that will ever be enough," responded Jerusha.

"Why not?"

"Well, for one of the three strikes-I left the faith. That's a big one!" she exclaimed. "And secondly, I violated my virginity, and aborted a living baby!"

Jerusha almost breathless, slumped over in the chair next to her bed. She was deeply troubled. Beth could see this, and suggested they postpone their talk until sometime next week. After all, they both had school studies and cheerleading obligations.

Jerusha lifted up her head, looked at Beth, and stated, "I need to tell you the third strike. The guy that I was intimate with is a Roman Catholic Gentile, the father of my aborted baby and a Hispanic."

Beth came over and gave Jerusha a hug. She promised that she would pray about this news, and promised they would talk more after the Bible study on Wednesday evening. "The Lord will work this out. You are His child now," Beth whispered softly into Jerusha's ear.

The decision was made. After much mental anguish, days of anxiety, and prayer regarding her parent's reaction to the news of the abortion, she decided to be up front with them, no matter the cost. But, how to do this was constantly on her mind. She would also share her decision to accept Christ as Savior.

Jerusha shared her decision with Beth, who believed she had made the right choice and she assured her of her prayers and assistance if she needed it.

All of this had been going on with Jerusha and Beth these last eight to ten days. After the Wednesday night Bible study, things came to, in a sense, a three-person committee meeting of Ryan, Beth, and Jerusha to answer the question-how to approach the situation?

All three settled into a back corner booth of the local fast food joint to hold their meeting. Beth reminded Jerusha that Ryan should be involved. After all, he was the father of the aborted baby, and had even financed the procedure. Beth believed that Ryan also needed to talk to his folks about his new belief, and the events in his life. It didn't take much persuasion. Ryan knew this was the right thing to do. In fact, Ryan, in his new-found belief, had become a new scholar in the Word. He was loaded with questions about becoming a Christian that would bring pleasure to the Lord in his daily life. Jerusha was not far behind in her studies of the Word. Beth was extremely pleased with both of their spiritual progress, and in so short a time it was evident that God's Spirit was at work in their lives.

"Look, why not just call our folks and talk to them about all this?" offered Ryan.

"You think that would do it for them. Wouldn't they ask questions that we didn't have the time to answer? I know my folks would…and…my brother and sister should know this. I don't want them to get it second-hand," responded Jerusha. "Yet," she continued, "calling them would be the easy way, wouldn't it Ryan?" She paused, took a sip of her soda, and looked down at the table. "I'm scared to death to face them."

"Me too," echoed Ryan.

Beth took it all in silently listening to the ongoing conversation. She was thankful to God that her life was an open book, especially to her family, friends, and co-workers. She knew she wasn't perfect, by any means, but the Lord had helped her to have a positive testimony for Him.

Beth had come to love these two new Christians, Jerusha and Ryan, especially Jerusha, who she now considered her to be the little sister she never had. Ryan, well, he's just a big, little brother, she thought while smiling in her mind.

The thought hit her, like a sudden, unexpected knock on a door. "Write them a letter," she said.

"Oh, that would be too long, and we couldn't answer their questions," retorted Jerusha.

"Yeah, that's right," agreed Ryan.

"No," stated Beth, "let me explain."

Jerusha and Ryan looked at one another with blank looks, masking their faces, and almost in unison said, "We're listening."

Beth then began to explain her plan. "Write letters to your folks saying you'd like to come home for awhile because there are some important things that have happened in your life since you have been at school. And let them know that letter-writing and phone calls are inadequate in sharing this information. That's the first step."

She continued, "The second step is for you both to arrange the same date with your folks, and you need to reveal everything. The third step is to prepare, prayerfully, what you will share with them when you actually meet them face-to-face."

Things were quiet among the three. They were digesting mentally Beth's plan. "It sounds good to me, how about you, Ryan?" questioned Jerusha.

"Count me in," Ryan replied.

'It had been a tough day.' Jerusha reflected as she tossed and turned trying to sleep. It was useless. So she relented, just laid there in bed, and went over in her mind, the activities of the day.

It all was so clear. She could see and hear herself talking to her parents with both Benjamin and Ruth sitting and listening in the background not uttering a word. She recalled the cheerful greeting they all exchanged with her. How much both Benjamin and Ruth had not only grown, but matured. Mother and dad, she thought, had not changed much, and they both seemed genuinely glad to see her. But the things she shared with them appeared to Jerusha, at least, that her parents were not at all happy with her. She could hear herself saying it, "Mom, dad, I'll make this short. Please let me finish it all before responding, okay?"

She could see that her dad was not too agreeable to this by just observing his reaction to what she said. Her mom, though, knew too many interruptions and questions would fracture what her daughter was going to tell them. She looked over to Jacob, who was about to object, "Look Jacob, let her be. Wait until she's finished. Is that asking too much?" Jacob saw the wisdom in that, and shook his head in a positive movement.

"All right, Jerusha," stated her mom, "tell us. We're all anxious to hear your news."

Jerusha hesitated, took in a deep breath. "After the prom last year, and a few months later, I realized that I was pregnant..."

Gasps filled the room. Jacob began to get out of his chair, Rachel looked sadly upon her perfect daughter, and then there fell a spontaneous silence across the room. Rachel motioned for Jacob to sit back down, as a tear slowly trickled down her cheek.

"I did wrong and I know it, and I was deeply ashamed," she continued. "I asked God to forgive me. I believe He did, but I was still pregnant, and did not know what to do. Marriage was part of the question, but with school and all, I wasn't sure that Ryan would want to get married. So I made another bad decision," she paused and began crying. Brushing away a tear she continued, "I had the baby taken care of." She couldn't say aborted-it was too brutal. Jerusha could not go on, she felt so shamed.

Rachel and Jacob both stood up from their chairs, while Benjamin and Ruth seemed to sink deeper into theirs.

Jerusha couldn't stop crying, which now had become more than her mother could handle. She rushed over to her daughter, stooped down, and hugged her passionately and cried, "Oh my daughter, my daughter."

Jacob just stood there. Great disappointment was expressed in every feature of his face. He stood there momentarily, then collapsed back into his chair, thinking 'how she could have shamed us so? They will put all of us out of the synagogue,' he mused!

All was quiet for awhile. They had all been shocked by this unexpected bad news.

Still sobbing and in the arms of Rachael, Jerusha said, "I'm so sorry for what I have done to you, and what I have done to God. Please forgive me if you can. I had to tell you, even though I knew it would hurt all of you," she hesitated to catch her breath. "But," she stammered, "since I've become a Christian, I could not keep this a secret. I had to apologize for my behavior because I love all of you dearly. The person who was instrumental in me making my decision to acknowledge Jesus as my Lord and Christ advised me that this was the right thing to do," she concluded with a deep sigh.

All of them could not believe what they had just heard Jerusha say. They were shocked. A Christian! They were all Jews, how could she?

Rachel had thought many times that Jerusha might come under religious teachings different from theirs as she went off to school. But she had hoped she would be faithful to the Jewish faith. She knew the cheerleading camps as well as the university had powerful influences on Jerusha's life, but this being a 'Christian' brought a spiritual division in their family.

"Jerusha," demanded Jacob, sitting up in his chair. "Who is the father of that baby?"

Before Jerusha could answer he stated, "Is it that Ryan boy. That Roman Catholic football- playing boy?"

Jerusha could barely look her dad in the face. His question brought back the shame of what she and Ryan had done that night, as well as the killing of her baby. "Yes, dad," she murmured, glancing up to look at him and then to Rachael.

Rachael frowned. "You could have told us," she said. "You know we would have been here for you, didn't you Jerusha? We would have forgiven you."

"Yes, Mom, but I was ashamed, still am, not only for me but for you. I didn't want you to know, even though I believe God and His Son, Jesus, have forgiven me for my shameful sins. But, I still have to live with the memory of them," she softly concluded.

"Jerusha," came a voice from the rear of the room. It was her brother, Benjamin, breaking the silence that had just settled among them after Jerusha's confession. "Why did you come here to tell us all of this?" he questioned, adding, "you could have kept it a secret, and no one but you and Ryan would have ever known. It would be the same as always, why? Now we have to live with it too!" concluded Benjamin defiantly.

"You are so right Benjamin. I'm sorry. I was going to do exactly what you said, you would never know, I would keep it a secret," she paused, looked around the room at her parents and Benjamin and

Ruth, who were eagerly hanging on her every word. "But when I became a Christian, all of that changed," she explained.

"A Christian, what is that?" blurted out Jacob. "We could forgive you those other things, but to turn your back on our faith. It's unforgivable!"

All was quiet in the room. It seemed to Jerusha that all of them were anticipating what her answer to dad would be. She did not know how to begin, but she had to explain. "Well, it happened one day when Beth and her boyfriend, Morey, who goes to the Coast Guard Academy, were having coffee with Ryan and I along with Melissa and Jake. You remember them?" she questioned. "Well, they were getting married, and were meeting with us to see if we would be in their wedding. Jake and Ryan were football buddies. Jake wanted Ryan to be the head usher, and invited me to be a bridesmaid.

"Whoa, wait a minute," interrupted Jacob. "What has all this got to do with being a Christian?" he impatiently requested.

"It leads up to it, dad," replied Jerusha. "I'll make it short." Jerusha continued her story. "We agreed to be in the wedding, both Ryan and I. That was settled but then out of the blue Jake asked if the pastor of the church Beth was attending would marry them. Beth said she wasn't sure, so he asked Morey if his preacher would marry them. Morey told them that he believed he would be willing to do that, if both Melissa and Jake were Christians."

Jerusha, raising her hand just above her head as if to announce something unusual, said, "dad, you won't believe this, but that is almost exactly what Jake said."

"Well, what was that?" responded Jacob. "What in the world is a Christian anyway?"

Jerusha quietly responded to her dad with encouragement from her Mom. "Jerusha, continue," urged her Mom. "We need to get on with this."

She didn't know for sure what was happening, but Rachael was having misgivings about what Jerusha was saying. It seemed deep down in her soul something special or different was going to happen to their family. She could feel it.

Jerusha continued, "Morey said a Christian is one who recognizes Jesus as Lord, and believes that He has risen from the dead, and calls upon Him to save him. Then he took a little New Testament from his pocket and turned to verses that told us what they meant."

Jerusha stopped, glanced around to Benjamin and Ruth and stated, "you know that mom and dad have told us the New Testament was for Gentiles, not us, so we have never even read it-any of it. But now I know it was written by Jews, all of it, except two books written by a Gentile who was a friend of the Jews. He read us these verses. I've almost memorized all of them. 'That if thou shalt confess with thy mouth the Lord Jesus, and shalt believe in thine heart that God hath raised Him from the dead, thou shalt be saved. For with the heart man believeth unto righteousness; and with the mouth confession is made unto salvation. For the Scripture saith, whosoever believeth on Him shall not be ashamed. For there is no difference between the Jew and the Greek: for the same Lord over all is rich unto all that call upon Him. For whosoever shall call upon the name of the Lord shall be saved.'"

"It was a revelation to me. Jesus is Lord, the resurrected Messiah! All I had to do was believe this truth about Him. That's the day I became a Christian," exclaimed Jerusha. "My life has not been the same since," she concluded.

"How can that be?" questioned Benjamin. "It's so simple."

"Yes, that's what so extraordinary about it, Benjamin, it's a gift-a gift of God. All one has to do is accept Jesus as God's gift to man. I learned that since I've been reading the New Testament and attending Bible study sessions at Beth's church."

"How can all of this be?" exclaimed Rachael. Meanwhile Jacob sat stuck in his chair, dumbfounded, unable to speak. Ruth was hearing everything! 'Boy,' she thought to herself, 'this has been some day!'

"Look, Mom, I've got this New Testament you can have it. Hopefully you will read it, but just let me read a few verses to you about Jesus," Jerusha pleaded.

"Okay, go ahead," spoke Benjamin, answering for his mother.

Then Jerusha open the red-bound New Testament, and began reading verses from Matthew and John. Matthew 1:21-23 "And she shall bring forth a son, and thou shalt call His name Jesus: for He shall save His people from their sins. Now all this was done, that it might be fulfilled which was spoken of the Lord by the prophet, saying, behold, a virgin shall be with child, and shall bring forth a son, and they shall call His name Emmanuel, which being interpreted is, God with us."

John 1:29 "The next day John seeth Jesus coming unto Him, and saith, Behold the Lamb of God, which taketh away the sin of the world."

Jerusha closed the book, and put it down on the coffee table next to her chair. The quietness in the room was deafening. No one uttered a word. It seemed that her reading had taken everyone's breath. Then from the rear of the room came some sniffing, even subdued crying. It was Ruth, desperately trying to remain quiet.

"What is it, Ruth?" asked Rachael, sensing her young daughters discomfort.

"It's all so confusing. I just don't understand all of this," replied Ruth, while drying her eyes.

"I know, honey," said Rachael in a comforting voice. She walked over to where Ruth was sitting, pulled up a chair and sat down next to her while giving her a hug. "We'll talk about this later."

"Yes, later," announced Jacob, who had been observing his family. "Jerusha, you can leave us now. You need to return to school," he suggested. "And we need to talk about all of this. What about Ryan? What's his situation?" he questioned, almost sarcastically.

Jerusha was a little taken aback by the bluntness of her dad's statement. She sensed that her dad did not have a favorable opinion of Ryan. But she did, and she was going to defend him now. "Dad, Ryan stood by me in this entire situation. He was willing to get married if it came to that. He did not know about the abortion, even though we had talked of the choices I could make concerning the baby. It was my choice!"

Jerusha was getting flushed in the face, just as she was when she told her family about the shameful things she had done earlier in their conversation. But now it was a face flushed in anger. "Ryan is a good guy," she continued. "We have grown closer through all of this; in fact, he became a Christian the next day after talking to Morey. Morey helped him understand what Jesus had done for him personally. Now, according to the Lord's Word, we are spiritual brother and sister in God's family. Ryan is at home now explaining all of this to his parents also."

With that said, Jerusha left the room. As she entered the vestibule she yelled back, "here are some booklets that tell you all about this. I'll put them on the table here under the mirror. Maybe you will have some time to read them."

Everything was back to normal, that is, college normal. Yet, for Jerusha and Ryan, it was not the same old normal. Things had changed for both of them, drastically, since becoming Christians. Their view of life had been given an entirely new perspective, as they continued to learn from the Sunday church service and Wednesday night Bible study.

They both had so many questions, and were so eager to learn all they could. Certainly the Holy Spirit was at work in their lives. The Bible was their most important textbook at the university, especially the Pauline Epistles, which addressed and answered practically all their contemporary questions.

Jerusha was having some questions that were not addressed at the church or the Bible study so she asked Beth if they could spend time together after cheerleading practice. Jerusha suggested a local coffee house where they could meet. She even insisted that if they did meet, she would be happy to treat.

Beth's schedule was really tight, but she reasoned that she and Morey had been instrumental in her salvation, as well as Ryan's. How could she refuse an opportunity to help Jerusha grow in the Lord?

Ryan happened to come into the coffee shop after football practice while Jerusha and Beth were meeting. "Hey guys, what's going on with you two?"

"Just have a short Bible study with some coffee," responded Beth, as she looked up to Ryan.

"Yeah, come join us," urged Jerusha. "I'm buying."

"It's hard to resist that offer. Do I need to have a Bible?" responded Ryan.

"We'll let you pass this time. Come sit there by Jerusha," Beth said.

Jerusha moved over in the booth to allow Ryan a place to sit. He sat down, but in doing so put his arm around her, hugged her for a moment, and then patted her on her head.

"What's this all about?" Jerusha questioned.

"It's for the coffee you're buying, for the study you have invited me to, and for just being you!" Ryan said, while looking into her eyes as if no one else was present in the entire coffee shop.

Jerusha could feel her face blushing, and she hoped no one would notice. She rarely blushed, but this was not something she could control. She thought to herself, 'how much Ryan has changed. Is God telling me something?'

"Well, what's the big study, Beth?" addressed Ryan. "I know you must be leading it."

"It's not a formal structured study, not like on Wednesday nights at church," said Jerusha.

"Yes," affirmed Beth. "We are doing more of a question-and-answer session on what the Bible says about certain things."

"Well," smiled Ryan. "What are the questions and the answers for today's session? I'm all ears."

"Are you serious, Ryan?" questioned Jerusha.

"Yes, I am," he replied. "Since I've become a Christian, I have a lot of questions I need answering. Yep, I'm serious. What's on today's menu, so to speak?"

"It is about the death of Christians and all of that," responded Beth, as she leafed through the Bible.

"Jerusha wanted to know where her baby is, and what will happen to believers when they die. For her it is all a new ball game, so we are going to see what God's Word has to say about all that."

"Are you interested Ryan?" she asked.

"I sure am. Fire away!"

Beth could see both Jerusha and Ryan were keenly interested in the topic, and began to turn to certain passages that support the truths she was about to share. "The person who calls upon the Name of the Lord for salvation is immediately baptized into the body of Jesus, His Church, of which He is the Head. The church, the Body of Christ, is not confined to any one assembly of believers. The church is a universal mystical body made up of all believers. This is found in I Corinthians 12:13." Beth then began to read the passage aloud. "For by one Spirit are we all baptized into one body, whether we be Jews or Gentiles, whether we be bond or free; and have been all made to drink into one Spirit."

Beth continued, "When you become a Christian, God adopts you as one of His children, as in Galatians 4:6-7…"and because ye are sons, God hath sent forth the Spirit of His Son into your hearts, crying, Abba, Father. Wherefore thou art no more a servant, but a son; and if a son, then an heir of God through Christ."

Beth continued in spite of the noise that was coming from the coffee shop. "Not only are we His children, but as I mentioned before, we are members of His Body which, is the true church of believers. And Jesus is the Head of all of us. This truth is found in Ephesians 1:19-23 and elsewhere," she explained.

"Look, Jerusha, why don't you look it up and read it to us? I don't have to read all this," she insisted.

Jerusha turned to Ephesians. She now knew where to turn to certain Books in the Bible, and if she didn't know where the Books were, she turned to the contents in the front of her Bible to locate them.

Ephesians was somewhat familiar to her because it contained some of the first verses after her conversion that really made an impression on her. She almost learned them from memory, but not quite verbatim yet. She went over it in her mind, "For by grace are you saved through faith; and not of yourselves: it is a gift of God." (2:8) She loved that verse.

"Well, read it, Jerusha," prodded Beth. Both Beth and Ryan were waiting.

"Okay," she said, and began to read. "And what is the exceeding greatness of His power to us-ward who believe, according to the working of His mighty power, which He wrought in Christ, when

He raised Him from the dead, and set Him at His own right hand in the heavenly places, far above all principality, and power, and might, and dominion, and every name that is named, not only in this world, but also in that which is to come: and hath put all things under His feet, and gave Him to be the head over all things to the church, which is His body, the fullness of Him that filleth all in all."

"Thanks, Jerusha," said Beth. She continued, "we are His family members, as well as His Church members whom He has saved from the penalty of our sins, which is spiritual death or separation from God. When we die, we will be with Him in Heaven. Let me read these verses that tell us about that. She turned to II Corinthians and read from chapter five verses one through 8. "For we know that if our earthly house of this tabernacle were dissolved, we have a building of God, an house not made with hands, eternal in the heavens. For in this we groan, earnestly desiring to be clothed upon with our house which is from heaven: if so be that being clothed we shall not be found naked. For we that are in this tabernacle do groan, being burdened: not for that we would be unclothed, but clothed upon, that mortality might be swallowed up of life. Now He that hath wrought us for the selfsame thing is God, who also hath given unto us the earnest of the Spirit. Therefore we are always confident, knowing that, whilst we are at home in the body, we are absent from the Lord: for we walk by faith, not by sight. We are confident, I say, and willing rather to be absent from the body, and to be present with the Lord."

"So when we die a physical death," she summarized, "we will be in the presence of the Lord, forever!"

Both Jerusha and Ryan had difficulty in holding back their tears. "What a great God we have," blurted out Ryan.

"Yes," echoed Jerusha. "How assuring it is to know we are the Lord's, and that we have Heaven waiting for us." She shifted around in the booth, took a Kleenex from her purse, and wiped away the tears staining her cheeks. After clearing her voice she said, "what about babies, Beth? It said nothing about them."

"You're right, Jerusha," assured Beth. "But, God covers all the bases. You see, unborn babies are not sinners, and even though the Bible says we are born in sin, unborn babies that are not born are taken into the presence of the Lord in a Heavenly body, to wait for the resurrection and the gift of a glorified body. For God is the Lord of the living and the dead." Beth stopped speaking. She was wondering if she was getting too deep for them. After all they are new Christians.

"What does a resurrected and glorified body mean?" asked Ryan.

"Isn't this enough for now, you guys?" countered Beth.

Both Ryan and Jerusha shook their head to the contrary.

"Okay, Ryan, but you get to read about it," she insisted.

At that, Jerusha pushed her open Bible over to Ryan. "It's your turn, big boy," she declared.

"Where do I go?" asked Ryan.

"Try First Thessalonians 4:13-18. It's about two-thirds of the way through the New Testament," guided Beth.

Ryan picked up the Bible, and instead of leafing through it he turned to the table of contents, and found it listed under page 1080. He turned there quickly, then looked to Beth and said, "What's that reference again?"

"Chapter 4:13-18. So go ahead read to us," she urged.

Ryan cleared his voice, and began to read slowly and carefully. "But I would not have you to be ignorant, brethren concerning them which are asleep, that ye sorrow not, even as others which have no hope. For if we believe that Jesus died and rose again, even so them also which sleep in Jesus will God bring with Him. For this we say unto you by the word of the Lord, that we which are alive and remain unto the coming of the Lord shall not prevent them which are asleep. For the Lord Himself shall descend from heaven with a shout, with the voice of the archangel, and with the trump of God: and the dead in Christ shall rise first: then we which are alive and remain shall be caught up together with them in the clouds, to meet the Lord in the air: and so shall we ever be with the Lord. Where comfort one another with these words."

Ryan finished reading. He paused, reflecting on what he had just read. "I've got to read that again," he uttered, and without waiting for the girl's approval, read all those verses over again. "That's fantastic!" he exclaimed.

"There's more," Beth said. "But I need to go. Perhaps you both can finish up here. You've got the check anyway Jerusha." Beth slid out of the booth, said goodbye and started out of the room.

"Wait, Beth," pleaded Ryan. "If it's alright with Jerusha, can we make it a threesome over coffee the next time?"

Beth turned back toward the booth, and looked at Ryan. "Sure, glad to have you join us. We will keep you informed." With that she turned toward the exit, and proceeded to leave the two in the booth with the Bible and their coffee.

CHAPTER 24

No Wedding

"There isn't going to be any wedding," announced Jerusha, as she put down her phone and yelled at Beth, who was washing her face in their bathroom.

"What are you talking about?" asked Beth.

"Melissa and Jake's wedding—remember we were to be in the wedding party?" replied Jerusha.

"But that's for a while yet."

"Doesn't matter now, does it?" questioned Jerusha.

"What happened?" as Beth retreated from the bathroom dressed and ready to go to their Bible study at their favorite coffee shop. (It was still light out, and they both enjoyed the sunset as they walked over to the café just a few blocks away. It was easier to walk than to drive, find a parking place—besides, they did not want to risk losing their parking place at the dorm.)

"Just sit down for a minute," urged Jerusha, "I'll tell you all about it. Jake has been put in jail, evidently for selling steroids. It looks like he is going to be there awhile. He has lost his scholarship, and probably any opportunity to go pro. The wedding is postponed for who knows how long." Jerusha was struggling to say the next sentence.

"What else Jerusha?" demanded Beth.

"She is thinking about aborting the baby," whispered Jerusha, agonizingly. "I tried to talk her out of it, but she's desperate now that Jakes in jail. No marriage, as well as her folks are not supporting her."

"Poor Melissa, poor Jake. Does Ryan know about this?"

"He probably does. Jake, at one time, was his best friend," concluded Jerusha.

"Well let's go then. We'll find out soon enough."

Ryan was already at the coffee shop. Three cups of coffee were on the table, along with his unopened Bible. With a smile, stretching from ear to ear, he got up, out of the booth, and said, "I thought you gals would be here before. What's kept you?"

"It's a long story," replied Jerusha.

"Here, sit down, both of you," urged Ryan. "Your coffees are all ready, and I might add, already paid for."

Beth slid into the booth and sat on the outer edge, leaving the seat across from her open for Jerusha and Ryan. They both followed suit, as Jerusha sat inside, leaving the outer edge available to Ryan. Immediately they all focused on their coffee, took a sip or two, as if to fortify them for their time of study. But instead of starting the study, there appeared to be something else on their minds.

Ryan put his coffee down and to the side as if to say, 'enough of that for a while,' and insisted that they tell him why there were late. "What's wrong?"

"I'll make it short. I got a call from Melissa just before we left the dorm," Jerusha sighed. "That's why we were late. There is not going to be a wedding!"

"Did she tell you why?" asked Ryan.

"Yes, because Jake was in jail for his involvement with steroid sales and distribution," explained Jerusha.

"Did you know that Ryan?" asked Beth.

Ryan shook his head in the affirmative, reached over to pick up his coffee, and took a few sips. He looked first to Beth and then to Jerusha, and motioned with his hand as if to plead innocent of withholding valuable information. After all, they, all three of them, had promised they would pray for Melissa and Jake that they would become Christians by putting their faith in Jesus as their Savior and

Lord. "He must have been involved in a plea bargain. That's why he is already in jail. And yes, I knew he was being arrested, but I didn't want to share this with you until I knew what was going to happen to him. You understand don't you?"

Neither Jerusha nor Beth replied. They just shook their heads and rolled their eyes, signaling a half-hearted acceptance of Ryan's plea.

"What's the situation with Melissa?" questioned Ryan.

"She's well along in her pregnancy and thinking about an abortion. We need to pray for her!" Jerusha said. She remembered when she was in that same predicament. The memories were not pleasant! Thank God, that was behind her and thank God she is forgiven. "I know that my baby is alive, in Heaven with my Heavenly Father." Then, she remembered Ryan. It was his baby also, and she remembered just after they became Christians and after many Bible studies, that Ryan had realized their forgiveness from God and the state of that aborted baby. This had drawn them closer to each other, and they had begun to feel a love for one another that Jerusha knew only God could have caused.

"Let's not forget Jake," remarked Ryan. Ryan was so thankful that he was not drawn into that sorry situation. He felt sorry for Jake, but Jake had had an opportunity to get out. He made the wrong choice. Yet, he was thankful to Jake for not implicating him. All of this was running through his mind at a furious clip. How thankful he was for Morey and Beth who had introduced him into a new life! A life that now had not only reason, but an eternal hope. That life also had an immediate hope in a person called Jerusha. God had something marvelous in store for them he believed, and hoped!

"Why don't we pray?" suggested Beth. They all bowed their heads, and one by one prayed. It was a tearful time of prayer, especially for Jerusha, since she had been through the same experience. 'I need to talk with her,' she thought.

Ryan was thinking the same thing about Jake. He needed to talk with him soon.

"Anybody need a refill," offered a sever standing next to their booth with a pot of coffee in one hand and decaf in the other. They all said 'yes,' but declined on the decaf.

"Look, we haven't even begun our study," stated Beth. "Let's make it short. Time is running. I just want to share one section of verses that is really terrible if one finds themselves in this situation. I'll read it, take note of it, and we will talk at our next study. Okay?"

There was silence from both Jerusha and Ryan. Beth took their silence to mean to continue. So, opening her Bible to II Thessalonians 1:7-12 she read: "And to you who are troubled rest with us, when the Lord Jesus shall be revealed from Heaven with His mighty angels, in flaming fire taking vengeance on them that know not God, and that obey not the gospel of our Lord Jesus Christ: who shall be punished with everlasting destruction from the presence of the Lord, and from the glory of His power; when he shall come to be glorified in His saints, and to be admired in all them that believe (because our testimony among you was believed) in that day. Wherefore also we pray always for you, that our God would count you worthy of this calling, and fulfill all the good pleasure of His goodness, and the work of faith with power: that the name of our Lord Jesus Christ may be glorified in you, and ye in Him, according to the grace of our God and the Lord Jesus Christ."

CHAPTER 25

Robert

Melissa aborted her baby. Jake supported the decision. It was a late term procedure. Both Melissa and Jake had already named the baby, but Jake saw that his situation was a long-term one, and Melissa knew her parents were not happy about her situation.

Yes, she aborted Robert. This was what they saw in a replay of the whole scene. Jeni, Robert, and One Fifty-Five had followed intensely the stories of the three couples. (Robert was still shaken from all that he had seen.)

Now it appeared to all of them that this tragic scene would be played before them again. But, there was no turning back. They wanted answers, and if it meant sitting and observing these procedures leading up to their murders, so be it. Even though they had not shared that verbally, it was an unmentioned agreement between them.

Melissa's procedure of the abortion was a duplication of Jerusha's procedure. Melissa was wheeled in to the surgical room, and assisted to lie down on the table. All the attendees were dressed in white garb. But this time the doctor took a large needle and injected it into Melissa's abdomen. He removed some fluid from the amniotic sac, and replaced it with salt water.

"That's not the same procedure One Fifty-Five went through, is it?" questioned Jeni.

"Doesn't look like it to me," offered Robert.

"Nor me," affirmed One Fifty-Five. He could not get his abortion nor Jeni's abortion out of his mind. He wondered if the killings bothered the moms of the babies. He shared his thoughts with Jeni and Robert.

"I think they answered that question for you One Fifty-Five," responded Jeni. "Remember their sorrow over the abortion? Especially after they became a Christian? They knew that the Lord Jesus had forgiven not only this sin, but all of their sins, past, present, and future, because they put their faith in Jesus."

"That's so right," echoed Robert. "We have learned so much. How Jesus loved and dealt with people down below. I'm sure this salvation message is in our Red-Covered Bible. We just haven't gotten to all that yet. Nor have we seen it on the Academy screen in the sessions we've been too," he concluded.

"Okay, that's right," expressed Jeni. "But let's get back to Melissa's story."

Robert pushed the play button, and immediately they were in the operating room with Melissa. The doctor had just removed the large needle from Melissa's abdomen. Everything appeared fine, even normal. But the baby, which they could not see, had his skin burned off. He was kicking and struggling violently to escape Melissa's womb. Finally as Melissa lay there, the baby died, convulsing, choking during the next thirty minutes.

Melissa stayed there, they could see, being attended to by some white-garbed people. Melissa went in to labor, and gave birth to a dead baby, covered in burns. The body was quickly incinerated.

"That was me, wasn't it?" Robert exclaimed and questioned all in one exhaled breath. He too was devastated. He was born dead! "That was my killing," he concluded, as he paused before the screen.

"But look," Jeni stated. "Down below we were dead. Up here we are alive!"

"Yes, Jeni, that's a wonderful reality," Robert said to her, "but I'm going to resume the story. You must be next," he reminded her.

"Give me your number, Jeni, and I'll push it in for you," requested Robert.

Slowly she spoke, "23,143,003."

Melissa returned home to live with her parents, who begrudgingly supported her until she could find a job and eventually become independent. Yet, Melissa struggled emotionally with the things in her life—the abortion of her and Jake's baby; the wedding that was called off; and Jake in jail.

Jerusha had talked with her on numerous occasions, even inviting her to church and an occasional college and career group meetings. But, Melissa had not accepted any of the invitations, and became increasingly reclusive. Nevertheless, both Jerusha and Beth prayed for her almost daily, because of their concern for her welfare.

Meanwhile, Ryan had visited Jake a few times in the local jail. Jake was waiting to be incarcerated in the state prison. Because he was a first time offender who cooperated with the local authorities, his sentence was reduced to three years, with the possibility of parole or early "good behavior" release.

This was encouraging to Jake, and his spirits were up when Ryan visited him. "How much longer will you be here?"

"Not much longer. Maybe a few days," responded Jake in a subdued voice.

This was not the usual bombastic Jake. 'Circumstances of late had their effects upon him,' thought Ryan. 'Yet he seems reconciled to his fate.' "Have you talked to Melissa since she was in the hospital?" queried Ryan.

"Yes, a few times. She's really down, and things are tough at home," he paused, drew in a big breath. "But we still hope something in the future will happen."

"How's that?" stated Ryan.

"I believe I love that gal. She's just right for me. I was going to marry her for the baby's sake, but I wasn't reluctant to do it. In fact, I wanted to get married. But now, well, you know." The visitation time was up. They announced this by blinking the lights a few times. This meant you had about two minutes left to end your visit. "I'll stay in touch," Ryan promised. "Let me know when you get transferred." He started to leave.

"Hey, Ryan, hold up," insisted Jake.

Ryan hesitated and turned back to Jake.

"How are you and Jerusha doing?" Jake asked.

"Well, it seems since we both became Christians, the Lord has bonded us. I'm going to present her with an engagement ring about the time that Beth and Morey get married. I'll keep you posted," he waved and turned to go.

"See ya," responded Jake.

Ryan stopped and went back to where Jake was sitting. He took a little booklet out of his back pocket. "I meant to give you this right-off, but forgot. It's the little booklet that helped me know the Lord. Here, take it and read it. It might be the same one that Morey gave you. I'll be praying for you."

With that he turned and exited through the nearest door. Jake sat there with that booklet, and stared down at it. 'Is this the thing that changed Ryan, almost radically?' He thought. 'Perhaps I should read it.'

CHAPTER 26

The Wedding

The time for the wedding was just around the corner. Beth wished it would be sooner, but with all the preparations, there should be more time. It was going to be a military-type ceremony, with some of Morey's buddies from the Academy. All the arrangements of travel, lodging, and all that goes into these affairs had to be considered. Thank the Lord, Beth reflected, that her mother and dad had taken care of all the arrangements, along with the bulk of the expenses. Morey's folks were also helpful taking care of necessary aspects of the event.

"Things going okay?" inquired Jerusha, as she and Beth left cheerleading practice headed back to the dorm. Both of them had been showering in their dorm instead of the gym. It was easier than in the locker room.

"As well as can be expected, especially since the wedding party has been firmed up," explained Beth.

"That's good."

"Yes, it is. Morey's brother will be the best man, and my sister will be my bridesmaid, and, of course, you are in it. Morey asked Ryan to be the head usher. They have become good friends, and e-mail a bunch," Beth concluded, as they approached the steps in front of the dorm. "Speaking of Ryan, how are you two getting along?"

Jerusha didn't respond but just smiled.

"I see you both together quite often. You both have become quite the couple on campus."

Jerusha blushed. Beth knew that since they had become Christians, she believed the Lord had begun a process in their lives of binding them together.

"Well, Jerusha, is that right?"

Jerusha blushed instantly, and spread into her beautiful radiant smile. "I've got to tell someone. You are my best friend, Beth, and I know you will keep our stuff private," she stated, and looked to Beth to get her nod of affirmation.

"Yes, certainly," affirmed Beth.

"Well then, we've become very intimate. Wait, that doesn't sound right. We have become very close emotionally, mentally, but most of all spiritually. I guess you would say we are in love or getting that way."

"That's great, really great. I've been praying for the both of you."

"And," interrupted Jerusha, "Ryan has changed his major to religion. Can you believe that? He thinks the Lord wants him to be a youth minister, a pastor, or even a missionary, or something along that calling. He's not sure yet, but he is sure the Lord is calling him to service."

"That's amazing," responded Beth tearing up. "What do you think about that?"

"If that is what the Lord wants, I'm all for it!" confirmed Jerusha.

Beth was amazed how Jerusha and Ryan had grown in the Lord. She was thrilled that she was a part of their spiritual experience and growth and felt a sense of thankfulness that God had allowed her to be involved in their lives. Jerusha had become her best friend in the process, another added blessing of God.

The wedding went well. It not only marked the union of Beth and Morey, who had waited four years for its fulfillment, but for both of them it marked the culmination of a college degree. As most weddings go, it was a happy occasion for all those who had worked so hard to make the event a success. They were glad it was behind them.

There was an incident at the end of the reception that Ryan and Morey had planned, with the agreement of Beth. (She was a bit reluctant with the idea at first, but she thought what a sweet thing it would be for her friend, Jerusha.) The plan was quite unique. Beth threw her bouquet, then Morey congratulated the recipient and announced for the couple's friends to come forward. As Ryan and Beth came up, along with other friends, Morey gave a small box to Ryan. He, in turn, turned to Jerusha, got down on one knee in front of her. Jerusha was dumbfounded, speechless, and overcome with emotion. The bystanders had grown quiet as if they had asked the question. "Will you marry me?" Ryan asked.

"Yes, certainly, yes," Jerusha answered. She took the box, took out the ring, and knelt down beside Ryan, and asked him to put the ring on her finger.

The place burst out with applause and laughter. Folks started coming to the newly- engaged couple with congratulations. Morey took Beth in his arms, he lifted her up, whirled her around as Jerusha and Ryan got up from the floor and stood arm in arm.

Morey and Beth were off on their honeymoon to Kauai in the Hawaiian Islands. Morey was assigned to a buoy tender in Kauai for the first two years of his Coast Guard service. Beth would apply for a teaching position on the island. They both were excited to be out of school and to be together. Morey would be at sea about two weeks out of each month checking on buoys around the islands. He would never be too far from home.

To Beth it was ideal, and now the four-year engagement period seemed like yesterday. Morey and Beth both wanted to begin a family and felt this was the time and place to make that a reality.

CHAPTER 27

Hawaii

'Kauai was Heaven on earth,' thought Beth. How blessed both she and Morey were. She had secured a part time job at the local high school as a physical education teacher and the coach of the cheerleading team. They found an ideal condo to rent in Kapaa, close to the ocean front, which was not far from the school, and close enough to the Coast Guard base in Nawiliwili Harbor. There was a minimal amount of travel, so they easily got by with their one little, compact automobile.

She was pregnant. What a wonderful thing for them! It was a month before Christmas, and she could already begin to feel the baby. She was due some time close to the end of February or beginning of March. Her doctor suggested she resign her position at the high school, and that was okay with her. Jerusha and Ryan were going to visit them during the holidays, so the timing was just right. Both Beth and Morey were anxiously waiting for their visit.

Beth and Jerusha had maintained contact constantly by e-mail and a few phone calls. Jerusha and Ryan planned to transfer to another university that provided more classes and a degree in his new major. It was a major that emphasized the Bible, and prepared him for various ministries. Jerusha would continue her career, at least for now, although they planned to marry before graduation. They would talk more of their plans upon their visit with Beth and Morey.

Christmas season was here, and it came quicker than both Beth and Morey had anticipated. Beth had gotten larger, and resigned her position at school. Morey kept going out on his weekly cruises through the islands.

Morey and Beth had to pick up their visitors at the airport. It was a happy reunion for all of them. Hugging one another, laughing, smiling and everyone talking at once amidst the traditional laying on of a beautiful lei of flowers to the first time visitors to the islands.

"Well, how was your trip?" asked Morey, as they made their way to the baggage claim area.

"Perfect, just perfect," responded Jerusha enthusiastically.

"Sure was," added Ryan.

"We are so glad to see you guys. We really missed you," exclaimed Beth, as they continued to look for their baggage in the claim area.

"Looks like you will be due soon," stated Jerusha.

"Not for about three more months hopefully," replied Beth.

They finally settled into the car, and drove off to their Kapaa condo.

"This place is gorgeous," declared Jerusha as she sauntered out on the open lanai to view the scene before her.

"Yes, it is. It's not ours, of course. It belongs to another Coast Guard couple who have been transferred to Alaska," stated Beth.

"It just worked out that our friends could not sell it, and we showed up in time to rent it—at a good rate, I might add," offered Morey. "The sunrises are something else," he bragged. "And the sunsets toward the Hanalei side of the island are spectacular!"

The condo was a two-bedroom, two-bath unit on the third floor. Jerusha was put into the guest bedroom with a limited ocean view, and Morey had rearranged the small office area into a makeshift bedroom for Ryan. After all, their visit would be two weeks—right through Christmas and New Year. Hopefully, Morey thought, this would be alright with Ryan. He wanted him to at least feel comfortable during their stay. The den had a view of a small mountain just outside Kapaa that looked like a sleeping giant.

Mealtime found both Jerusha and Ryan moved in to their rooms, but anxious to go beaching, which was planned to take place right after they had eaten something. "If you don't mind me asking, Jerusha, how is your family? And Ryan, yours also?" Beth asked.

"Yes, if it's okay with you guys, fill us in. We have been praying for both your families," echoed Morey.

"Sure, why not?" exclaimed Jerusha.

"No problem," concluded Ryan. "We are both family outcasts! When Jerusha and I announced our engagement, it seemed that it was the final blow to our families. They are struggling with the fact that we both became Christians. The prospect of having an ex-Roman Catholic married to an ex-Jew as son-in-law or daughter-in-law is beyond their religious tolerance."

"Yes, it has really been a cause of concern to say the least," added Jerusha. "We are praying for some kind of a break in both of our families for the things we did that hurt them deeply. Only God can work that out," she sighed.

"We've sent them information on how to become a Christian, but I'm not sure they have read any of it!" interjected Ryan.

"Well, that's not good news," responded Beth. "It looks like things got worse with your engagement, doesn't it?" she questioned.

"That's for sure," responded Jerusha and Ryan simultaneously.

"Well look, let's finish up and hit the beach," announced Morey.

"But wait, before we go, what's new with Melissa and Jake?" Beth asked.

"Nothing is new. Everything is the same. Melissa is at home—not much change emotionally, and Jake is in the state prison. No good news there either!" answered Jerusha.

With that said, they all left the table, put the dishes in the sink, and prepared to hit the beach.

The whole Hawaiian experience had been beyond Ryan's and Jerusha's expectations.

Waimea Canyon, the Grand Canyon of the Pacific, was awesome with high mountainous terrain divided by narrow canyons, cliffs, and waterfalls. After stopping at many of the overlooks to the canyon, they decided to have lunch at the small restaurant in Kokee Park. They enjoyed the meal, museum and gift shop, as well as a stroll into the picnic area. They were amused at all of the chickens that were running free. They learned they were called 'jungle fowl' and were descendants of Hawaii's early settlers.

After lunch they drove down the mountain back toward Kapaa, which would take them about an hour, depending on traffic. They all settled into the car for the return trip. (Morey was not with them as he had to be on duty, but since he had been there several times already, they decided to go without him.) "I missed Morey not being with us today," spoke Beth, from the back seat behind Ryan who was driving. Beth sat there purposely so she could talk with Jerusha who she could see from her view from the back seat. They were all belted up.

"Yeah, I wish he was here also," agreed Ryan. "He knows these roads better than I. They are really curvy and somewhat hairy."

"Just keep watching the road Ryan," encouraged Jerusha. "No more sightseeing while you drive," as she gently tapped him on the shoulder.

They were coming down a pretty steep grade, and Jerusha could see that it bottomed out with a turn to the right. "Slow down a bit Ryan," she urged. "There's a curve ahead." "Okay," replied Ryan.

"Look, there's that rim-view road on which we came. Remember it connects to this road." Jerusha cautioned.

"Yeah, that's it. That was a wild drive, for sure!" remembered Ryan.

Just then, as he was making the turn, a pick-up truck came barreling out of the rim road, and smashed into the rear of the car, just where Beth was sitting. The car was sent spinning from one side of the road to the other until it smashed into a rocky cliff on the side of the highway. The truck headed toward a grove of trees across the highway' sliding head first into the dense forest.

They were all in the hospital. Ryan and Jerusha were fine. A bit shaken up, yet okay. Their concern was for Beth. She remained unconscious even now, after they all had been air- lifted to the emergency room to Lihue Hospital. Beth was pretty broken up, and she was in critical condition in the intensive care unit.

The driver of the truck was also in intensive care. He was the only one in the vehicle which probably accounted for him missing the stop sign, as he evidently was more interested in sightseeing than paying attention to his driving.

Morey's buoy tender was docked in Oahu for its monthly checkup, and he was on board when his commander contacted him about the accident and Beth's condition. He hopped the next plane out of Honolulu, and was at the hospital within the hour. He met Ryan and Jerusha in the waiting room. He could tell that they had both been crying. "We have been praying, Morey." Jerusha whispered in his ear, as she hugged him.

"The doctor wants to talk with you as soon as you get here," announced Ryan, pointing to the door to the intensive care unit. "Just go in," urged Ryan. "We will wait here."

Morey immediately headed for the door. As soon as he entered the room, he saw Beth surrounded by nurses and doctors working on her. He could see she was unconscious. One of the doctors noticed Morey coming into the room and headed toward him. "Are you this lady's husband?" he asked as he approached with an extended hand. "I'm Dr. Brown," he continued, as they shook hands.

"What about her and the baby? I came as soon as I could."

"They are both alive," he offered, "but the situation is not good. Your wife has sustained numerous injuries, with a fractured spine near the hip region, a few broken bones in the arm and shoulder area, and she is suffering from internal bleeding."

Morey was stunned. 'How could this happen?' he asked himself, as he petitioned the Lord for His help and strength.

"Mr. Dawson, are you all right?" questioned the doctor as he guided Morey to a nearby chair insisting he sit down.

"Doctor, what needs to be done? Please be truthful with me," he pleaded.

"I do not believe we can save both of them," acknowledged the doctor. "They are both badly damaged. We could lose both of them. Your wife cannot sustain her own life, and the life of her baby girl."

Morey felt like he was in a fog. He heard the doctor, even understood all that he had said, but it all seemed like a dream.

"If we tried to birth the baby, I do not believe the baby would survive outside of the womb. But if we operated now, we could perform a Caesarian procedure, and take the baby from the womb. But we are still not sure the baby would survive. It would greatly increase your wife's chances of survival," concluded the doctor. "We have an urgent situation here, and we must proceed as soon as possible."

Morey, although still in shock, understood the doctor's explanation. He prayed silently as the doctor waited for some sort of reply. He knew the situation was urgent.

Morey's thoughts cleared. He knew the Lord had given him some insight. 'The baby, their little girl, will be with the Lord, and Beth will continue to be my wife. Some day there will be other children in our lives. Baby Jeni would be guaranteed a home in Heaven, secure and eternal.' Beth and he still had a future in the Lord's service. "Doctor," Morey said with a tear drenched face, "please save my wife."

"He made a choice," admitted Jeni. "It was my life or my mom's life." Robert, Jeni, and One Fifty-Five continued to watch what was going on in the hospital's operating room.

The doctor performed the Caesarian to take out the baby, but the little girl was dead.

"How's the mother?" asked one of the assistants.

"All her vital signs are positive. Let's begin to treat her injuries as best we can," as all of the medical team began to focus on Beth.

"Are you all right?" questioned One Fifty-Five. There was no answer.

"Pause the screen Robert, will you?"

"Jeni," repeated One Fifty-Five, speaking louder. "Are you all right?"

"He had to make a choice, didn't he? It was either Beth or me. And that decision was my killing!" She hesitated, "but I know it was caused by an accident, a terrible accident. If there had not been that accident up there on that mountain, I would have been alive down there on Earth even now," she surmised with a heavy sigh.

"That's probably right," assured One Fifty-Five, "alive and loved!"

"It was the right decision," Jeni shared thoughtfully.

They all remained silent, reflecting upon all they had viewed on that giant screen frozen before them. No stirring occurred. They were immersed in their thoughts. It had been a taxing time for all of them.

Through all of this, their Erics had not appeared. Did they know what was going on in the Celestrial Library with their charges? One Fifty-Five brought up this question to the group.

"I think they knew," said Jeni, regaining her composure. She spoke on, "they wanted us to know about our killings, and we just found out! This story is not over. Let's see what else happens."

"Sounds good, let's do it. Press the button Robert," urged One Fifty Five.

It was almost a year since that horrible accident on the canyon road. Beth had recovered to some normalcy, after being in a body cast for many unbearable, unending days. If it hadn't been for Jerusha and her constant care, Beth didn't think she would have been able to handle the loss of her baby, nor the multiple injuries and surgeries that she had endured.

Beth had relied on her faith in Jesus Christ as her strength, as well as many of the Promises in God's Word. II Corinthians 1:3-4 were of particular comfort, and she had memorized them early in her rehab. She would reclaim them many times. "Blessed be God, even the Father of our Lord Jesus Christ, the Father of mercies, and the God of all comfort: who comforteth us in all our tribulation, that we may be able to comfort them which are in any trouble, by the comfort where with we ourselves are comforted of God."

Not only was the Lord with me, reflected Beth, but beyond a doubt, God had sent Jerusha to be her comfort. 'Praise Him,' she said silently, while thanking Him for Jerusha. She helped her through her recovery, and perhaps even secured her sanity.

Jerusha had not only been her nurse, her companion, and housekeeper but her dear and close sister in the Lord.

Beth remembered well the day that she had been brought home from the hospital. Morey got her all set up in a bed overlooking the ocean. He made it as comfortable for her as she was encased in that body cast. After all, her spine had been broken in more than one place.

"You okay?" asked Jerusha.

"Yes, I think," replied Beth, with a grimace.

"Look, before we get started with more conversation," interrupted Morey in a kind voice.

"Yes, what?" queried Beth.

"Hmm, I need to run this by you before you rest,"

"Well, what is it, Morey?"

"As you know, Ryan has gone back to school," he paused, "but Jerusha is still here. The three of us met, and Jerusha and Ryan, after praying, suggested that Jerusha stay with you until you were fully recovered, or close enough to be left alone, especially since I am on sea duty most of the time."

So that was it. For almost a year, Ryan was in school, and Jerusha had spent a school year with Morey and Beth as her nurse and big sister. Jerusha did get to be the part-time cheerleading coach at the high school, replacing Beth temporarily.

―

Beth and Morey were alone. Jerusha had gone back to the Mainland. Beth had grown to love her friends over the past months. Jerusha and Ryan were like a sister and brother. How thankful she was for their Christian friendship. How thankful she was for their Christian testimony to her and Morey. They truly were a lasting testimony to the grace of God!

―

"I told you we would find them here," Eric said to the two Erics beside him as they approached the auditorium. One Fifty-Five was talking as they entered the room. The threesome stood up from their seats, surprised and startled that their Erics were there. The screen was still playing, but no one was paying attention now.

"One Fifty-Five," Eric looked to him, and asked him to turn off the screen.

"Why?" said Jeni. "We wanted to see what was going to happen to us."

"You have probably seen enough," responded Jeni's Eric. "Besides, remember, we told you that you can only view up to yesterday down below."

"We need to leave right now," Robert's Eric spoke in a voice close to a command.

"What's the hurry, anyway?" asked One Fifty-Five.

"All three of you are going on a divinely-appointed trip. You can't be late."

"A Divinely-appointed trip? Where to?" questioned Jeni.

"It is a trip that will change your eternal life forever. One you will never forget. All of you are going below to a meeting with the Lord in the clouds. I can hear the trumpet sound," declared Eric. "It's time to go!"

www.ingramcontent.com/pod-product-compliance
Lightning Source LLC
LaVergne TN
LVHW021711060526
838200LV00050B/2614